A DARK FATE

NORTHERN WITCH #5

By K.S. Marsden

To Paula

Happy Reading

K.S. M

Northern Witch

Winter Trials (Northern Witch #1)

Awaken (Northern Witch #2)

The Breaking (Northern Witch #3)

Summer Sin (Northern Witch #4)

A Dark Fate (Northern Witch #5)

ISBN: 9798843342548

Chapter One

"More children are missing..."

The announcement was in a dull tone. Another disappearance, no clues, and fading hope. What must the newest parents be feeling? They had been mere witnesses to the worst happening to other families, and now they were in the middle of a nightmare.

"That brings the total to five missing."

Mark's friends were all shades of grey, hovering in formal clothes at a vigil for the missing kids. Only his boyfriend was in colour, but as Damian turned to him, his blue eyes faded to black.

"You're looking in the wrong place, Mark." Said the demon within...

Mark jerked awake, his arm aching from Harry's punch. He squinted in the bright summer light. "What?"

"It's the first time I've seen you in a week. I've only got half an hour's dinner break, and you're gonna sleep through it?"

"Some of us don't get the luxury of a nine-to-five. I'm up at dawn to do the proper work." Mark yawned. He'd started working at Mr Brown's dairy farm, as he did every summer for the last four years. He'd never been this tired before, the dregs of dark magic he'd used was still sapping his strength. The withdrawal not letting him sleep at night.

Mark felt a sickening tremble in his hand, and shoved it in his coat pocket, out of sight.

"Sorry, what did I miss?"

"The pro photographer has posted the Prom photos on their website." Sarah announced with a grin, shoving her phone in Mark's face.

Mark obediently looked through the gallery, flicking between photos of his classmates, awkwardly posing in formal attire.

Mark paused as he saw one of him and Damian. Mark looked a bit of a mess in his ill-fitting suit; but his boyfriend looked amazing, even with the bruises that had cast his face in shadow.

A giddy warmth surged through him. That was the night when Damian had first told him that he loved him...

"When are you next seeing Damian?" Sarah asked, smiling at his moment of gooiness.

"He's still at footie camp, but he's gonna be back in time for the Solstice tomorrow."

Damian had scored a dream job for the summer holidays – an assistant coach for the junior football club. They had started the summer with a team-building camp at Dalby Forest, and Mark hadn't seen Damian in days. He was itching to have his boyfriend back at his side.

"Good, you can invite him to my set in Sheffield on Saturday." Harry nudged Mark.

Mark blanched. "Saturday. Sheffield." He repeated, hiding that he'd completely forgotten.

"Then there's Thirsk on Wednesday, and Cawood the following Friday." Sarah rattled off, knowing her superstar's itinerary by heart.

"Three gigs in one week?" Harry asked weakly. "Don't y'think that's a bit much? I need to rest my voice."

"Hmm, good point. I've also had some interest from BBC Introducing... might be best to save your voice for them." Sarah pushed to her feet. "I'll call Thirsk to cancel."

Mark watched her walk away, phone stuck to her ear. "I didn't realise you'd signed up to *BBC Introducing* – that's massive!"

"Well, my manager signed me up." Harry shrugged. "Chances are nowt will come of it."

"Don't sell yourself short, you're an amazing singer. And you heard Sarah, there's already interest..." Mark's voice trailed off. He knew his best friend better than anyone, and he could tell that Harry wasn't as excited as he was. "What am I missing?"

"Nowt, nowt. It's a dream come true. What I've always wanted." Harry sighed. "Don't mind me, I'm just tired."

"Uh-huh." Mark wasn't convinced. "Y'know you can always talk to me. About owt."

"Cheers mate, but I'm fine." Harry plastered on a fake smile. "Better than fine. Haven't you heard, I'm on track to be a star. I best get back to work."

Harry clapped Mark on the shoulder, and jumped up from the bench, heading back to the coffee house that employed him for the summer.

*****

Mark cycled to Denise's house. He'd been putting off the visit for the last couple of weeks, ever since Silvaticus betrayed him and trapped Damian in a demon prison. Mark's stomach roiled at the thought of his sweet and gentle boyfriend being stuck in that awful place. His only reprieve was Robert, the unlikeliest hero, had kept Damian unconscious throughout the imprisonment and torture.

Mark took a deep breath and knocked on Denise's door.

Denise appeared, her hair a bright, freshly-dyed yellow. "Ah, I was wonderin' when you'd turn up. Cuppa?"

Without waiting for an answer, Denise turned back into her house, shuffling towards the kitchen.

Mark followed obediently, closing the door behind him. "Sorry I didn't come sooner. I didn't know how... I was recovering..."

Denise glanced up from the tea tray, with a knowing look. "I don't blame you if you don't forgive Danny for his part. Not straight away. You both have your hearts in the right place; it's frustrating that demons are messin' with our witches."

Mark felt a flush creep up his neck. Denise seemed to have read his thoughts, and now he felt guilty for not hurrying to embrace his fellow-witch. "How is Danny?"

"Devastated. Silvaticus betrayed him too, after everything Danny did to try and help him and Eadric." Denise sighed. "He's locked up in the garage at the mo, if you want to see him."

"Really?"

"Yeah, he thought being out in the middle of nowhere was safer than at his flat in town. Until we work out how much of a threat Silvaticus poses..." Denise nodded towards the garden. "We've turned the garage into a mini apartment; and Nanna's organised some of the coven to watch him."

Mark bit his lip. He kept forgetting how much Nanna seemed to take care of, and so effortlessly. Part of him was worried she was pushing herself too much, especially after her recent collapse... part of him worried how he'd ever manage even half of what she did, when Mark officially took over.

After he finished his cup of herbal tea, Mark made his way to the garage, his feet slow and heavy. He passed Denise's living room, and spied a couple of witches from the coven watching TV. Mark gave them a brief wave and carried on outside, aware of their eyes following him.

Mark knocked on the door.

"Yeah." A faint reply came.

He took a deep breath and let himself in. Last time he'd seen the garage, it had been a makeshift gym. Now, it had a sofa bed, that was a mess of blankets and sheets. There was also an old armchair, and a stack of books next to a silent TV set.

Danny had changed too, Mark had never seen him look so haggard. His hair was a ruffled mess, and his chin sported a couple of week's growth, the beard uneven and patchy. The smart, sharp clothes Danny always wore were replaced with a rumpled navy tracksuit.

Mark's stewing anger towards the young man faded, to be replaced by pity. It looked like Danny was punishing himself, more than any official justice could do.

The history teacher stared at Mark, his surprise overcoming his self-loathing for a few brief minutes. "What are you doing here? I mean... I wasn't expecting you."

Danny made a futile attempt to straighten his appearance, looking thoroughly embarrassed.

"I came to see how you're doing..." Mark said quietly.

"Why?" Danny frowned. "Oh, right, the friend thing."

Mark took a deep breath, he'd forgotten how annoying Danny was, even without the demons and betrayals. "I need to know what happened. I thought demons couldn't lie, but Silvaticus broke his promise, about keeping Damian safe."

"Ah, that's more like it. I thought the friendship thing was a ruse." A familiar, patronising look crossed Danny's face. "Demons can't lie. You have to consider what Silvaticus said, very carefully."

Mark racked his brain, going back to when they had gone on their mission to the demon prison, to stop the hell beasts from chasing Robert. Silvaticus had *helped* him... Mark's blood ran cold, and goosebumps raised on his arms. He was a dolt; a trusting, foolish dolt.

Silvaticus had done exactly as Mark asked – he'd called off the hell beasts – he'd said nothing about stopping the demons from hunting Robert with other methods...

Silvaticus had also been very careful to say that *he* would not harm Damian. Mark chewed his lip; how could he have overseen the hole in that promise

– he'd been an idiot to assume that meant Damian was safe from *all* demons.

"Yes, well... as long as you learn from your mistakes." Danny said in a snooty teacher tone, but his expression darkened. "Silvaticus fooled me, too. So really, *you* had no chance against him."

Mark tried not to rise to Danny's unintended ribbing, but his earlier sense of pity was starting to fade. Mark knew that no one deserved this; but he couldn't help thinking that it wouldn't hurt for this arrogant git to be taken down a peg or two. "These demons have been around for millennia; they've got plenty of practise manipulating humans."

Mark wondered whether Robert's newest move was just that – a practised play in a game too big for Mark to comprehend. But Mark sensed that even the demon was surprised that he'd shared his real name with the witch, essentially putting himself at Mark's mercy. Yet... that could just be part of the underhanded play. Mark was going to take Harry's advice – he was never going to trust a demon again.

"Silvaticus made me feel like I wasn't alone; for the first time in my life, someone understood me." Danny said quietly, picking at his frayed tracksuit sleeve. "Silvaticus showed me that we had so much in common, he really opened my eyes to who and what I am."

Mark sat silently, not quite following what the other witch was saying. Luckily, Danny didn't seem to need him to take part in the conversation.

"I... I've never understood relationships. I've never felt a drive to connect with people on that level before. I figured that I just hadn't met the right girl, yet, and maybe things would change once I did. But... I'm just getting left further behind."

"You're ace?" Mark blurted out.

"Thanks, you're swell too." Danny frowned, the terminology going over his over-inflated head.

"No, ace as in 'asexual'."

"That's what Silvaticus calls it." Danny nodded slowly. "Do you... d'you think that's why I... am the way I am?"

"No, I've met loads'a nice ace people. You bein' a git is all you." Mark snorted, unable to help it. "Trust me, your sexuality doesn't define your character."

"It seems that I have a lot to learn." Danny scratched at his scraggly beard. "Thank you for coming. Even if I don't show it, I appreciate you being here."

Mark shrugged. "That's what friends do."

Chapter Two

By the time Mark got home, he was jittery with fatigue. His very bones were aching; but he knew that if he tried to sleep, it would just be another restless night.

As he cycled up the drive, Mark smelt a familiar, sweet smell. He sighed and headed into the back garden, where Michelle was sitting in the sun, casually smoking as she scrolled through her phone.

Michelle offered Mark the joint, and he plucked it from her fingers. He'd previously been wary and a little disgusted at her use of weed; but Mark had to admit that Michelle was right – it took the edge off his cravings for dark magic.

He dropped onto the bench next to her and took a drag. Mark coughed as the fumes hit the back of his throat – he was still such a rookie.

"Have you seen, the photographer has posted prom pics." Michelle said, angling her phone towards Mark.

Mark caught a glimpse of Michelle in her black dress, her very dazed date at her side, looking at her with dopey eyes.

"Yeah, Sarah showed me." Mark replied. "How's things going with Peter?"

"I think he saw prom as this monumental shift in our relationship, and he's ready to be soulmates..." Michelle shrugged. "Whereas I saw it as just a bit of fun. He's good in all departments, but he doesn't compare to..."

"Robert." Mark finished, when Michelle trailed off.

"You think I'm pathetic." Michelle muttered.

Mark glanced at the ex-bully. "Does it matter what I think?"

"No, it bloody don't." Michelle snapped back to her usual level of bitterness.

Mark didn't think he'd ever get used to the fact that his *cousin* used to date the demon that possessed his boyfriend. *Date* was probably too innocuous a word, but Mark didn't want to think about the nitty or gritty.

"What the 'eck are you smokin' that crap for?" Nanna's voice thundered over the garden, laced with concern.

"Um..." Mark shoved the joint guiltily back to Michelle, as Nanna walked towards them, laden with shopping bags.

"I'm positively insulted." Nanna shook her head. "Denise grows much better marijuana than this cheap shit. You should have picked some up today."

Having said her piece, Nanna lugged her shopping inside, leaving her bewildered grandkids alone.

"I was not expecting that." Michelle sniggered. "Do you ever get used to her?"

"No, never." Mark said, he didn't know if he even wanted to get used to Nanna's eccentricities. She always kept them on their toes. "I'm just going for a private word with Nanna. You're... staying here, right?"

Michelle made a non-committal sound and returned her attention to the photos on her phone.

Whilst she was temporarily distracted, Mark ducked inside, following the sound of rattling jars to Nanna's kitchen.

"They didn't have any spaghetti hoops, so I got you the plain stuff..."

"You haven't told her yet." Mark said quietly.

Nanna paused, hand resting on the cupboard. "I aint found the right time."

"Rubbish."

Nanna sighed. "How am I supposed to just drop this on her? After all she's been through?"

"Are you kidding me? All Michelle has ever wanted is to find her real family. She's gonna be thrilled..." Mark paused, thinking of the volatile girl. "Eventually..."

"Hmph."

Mark sat down at the kitchen table and took a deep breath. "I don't want to take the Grand High Witch powers at the Solstice tomorrow."

"Are you still struggling from the withdrawal?" Nanna asked, her eyes dropping to Mark's trembling hands.

Mark clenched his fists, embarrassed at the continued physical weakness. "That's part of it, but... I don't want to assume the role, until Michelle knows everything."

21

"You want to hand it over to Michelle?" Nanna frowned. "She's got the potential to be a powerful witch, but I don't think she's stable enough for this responsibility."

"No... I mean, maybe." Mark shook his head. "I want to be open and honest about this. Michelle has been lied to, and kept from her heritage her whole life. I don't want to stitch her up again – wait until after I've inherited the title and *then* say 'oh, by the way, you were an heir too'."

"Fine, we'll postpone the transfer until Lughnasadh. That still gives you a month to adapt to your new powers, before college starts."

"Deal." Mark said, getting up from his chair. "But don't use that as an excuse to delay further – you're telling Michelle now, or I am."

*****

Mark had been roped into building the bonfire for the Summer Solstice party. It towered to an impressive height, to provide light and warmth for the witches and their families.

Nanna had already rang round the coven, and told them that their witchy skills would no longer be needed tonight. Mark didn't know if it was just his imagination, but he thought some of the senior coven members were relieved that he wasn't taking over from Nanna yet.

This evening was the first time Mark had seen most of the coven since Nanna's little announcement, and it made him all the more aware of how young and untrained he was.

Mark was grateful to see Damian arrive with his Aunt Maggie, knowing they would be on his side. He felt a jolt of surprise when he saw Maggie's girlfriend in tow. Only a couple of weeks ago, Maggie had learnt the hard way that her nephew was possessed by a demon. And that everyone already knew.

If she was here with her girlfriend, it meant Maggie and Miriam were trying to sort things out. Mark couldn't help feeling a little guilty for the part he played in the subterfuge.

Damian's eyes locked onto Mark, and he marched up the hill to him. His blue eyes sparkled mischievously, and without a word, he grabbed Mark's hand and pulled him into the garage.

"Happy six-month anniversary." Damian said, biting his lip.

"Happy anniversary." Mark echoed. Suddenly realising Damian was right.

It was six months exactly since they shared their first kiss in this very shed. Mark wondered if –

Damian leant forward and kissed him, tender and loving.

Mark's hands crept up to Damian's neck, pulling him deeper.

"Mark!"

Mark groaned at the sound of his best mate's voice. "Déjà vu."

Damian chuckled, pressing his forehead against Mark's.

"What?" Mark demanded.

"Nowt, just wanted to let y'know we're here. Big night an' all." Harry shrugged.

Sarah looked embarrassed on behalf of them both. "Sorry Mark. Sorry Damian."

"S'fine." Mark replied, reluctantly disentangling himself from Damian. "Actually, the big night has been postponed 'til August."

"Why?"

"I just… haven't recovered enough from using dark magic." Mark said, figuring that was the only part he could share, whilst Michelle was still in the dark.

"Hmph." Harry's expression froze. It was no secret how he felt about Mark's continued dubious choices.

"You alright?" Damian asked, his brow crinkling with concern.

"Yeah, believe it or not, Michelle has been helping me." Mark said. "I think she kinda likes lording over me, that she's an *ex*-addict."

"Wow, she's come such a long way, these last few months." Sarah said, honestly happy for the school bully.

"Shall we go out to the party?" Mark asked, shooing his friends out of the garage, before they could ask any more questions about his secret cousin.

~~~~~

A pick-up truck pulled into the crowded driveway, and two ridiculously-handsome men walked up, causing many a person to stop and stare.

The older guy was Nanna's sort-of boyfriend; the new farrier that had caused such a stir in the horsey circles. Beside him, Mark vaguely recognised his nephew, the original 'hot-farrier', clearly returned from his stint in the US.

Mark wondered if that meant Derek would leave, as he'd only been covering his nephew's clients temporarily.

One person who seemed less-than-thrilled about these guests was Nanna herself. Mark was surprised to see her freeze at the sight of her boyfriend. "What are you doing here? I didn't invite you."

"I know." Derek replied, his eyes narrowing slightly. "I saw your son in town – he was shocked you hadn't mentioned the biggest party of the summer and invited us."

"He had no business... I'm uninviting you..." Nanna replied, more flustered than Mark had ever seen her.

Derek looked dazed and hurt by her response. "Do you want me to leave?"

"Yes... No... It's a free country, you can do what you want." Nanna snapped, throwing her arms in the air and storming away from her lover.

"What was all that about?" Damian asked warily.

"Haven't the foggiest..." Mark replied.

Derek's nephew gave him a very hearty pat on the shoulder. The two farriers slunk away, to join the rest of the party goers, soon falling in with the other adults.

Later in the evening, Mark's Dad roped Mark and his friends into ferrying the food from the barbeque to the trestle tables.

Mark manoeuvred the latest plate of sausages onto the over-crowded table, wondering what would be faster – his freeze spell, or the plate of burger buns that tilted precariously on the edge of the table…

Mark looked up as someone else caught the tipping plate.

Miriam straightened the plate, then helped herself to some food, doing her part to demolish the edible mountain.

"Hey, looks like you're back in Aunt Maggie's good books." Mark said. His positive tone not quite natural. "I'm… um… sorry for my part in what happened. I shouldn't have let Damian keep his secret for so long."

"Thanks." Miriam gave him a patronising look. "But that's not necessary. You and Damian are just kids, our relationship shouldn't be your concern. I made the choice to keep Damian's secret at any cost, and I would do it again."

Mark stood dazed for a moment – Miriam always managed to surprise him – she was distant and kept herself to herself, but she was a very good person underneath.

"Thanks. Is there owt I can do t'help?" Mark asked.

"Damian's vocally defending my actions at home." Miriam shrugged. "This can't be fixed by magic, no matter how much I wish it could."

Having said her piece, Miriam took two plates of food back to her girlfriend.

Mark watched as Maggie took the offering, overly polite in her thanks. The two women then stood stiffly next to each other; their relationship drama clear for all to see.

Mark sighed, between those two, and Nanna and Derek's odd behaviour earlier…he just couldn't work out what was wrong with adults. They were supposed to be grown-ups, they were supposed to have everything figured out; and here he was with a healthier relationship with his demon-possessed boyfriend!

"What are you smirking at?" Damian asked, popping up with the next load of chicken wings.

"Just glad I'm me – and that I've got you." Mark replied honestly, making his fella smile in return.

The party went on well into the shortest night, and it was past midnight when people started to leave.

Mark had survived, and the rest of the coven had been… not completely embracing of their new leader-to-be; but at least civil.

Mark knew that he couldn't waste a minute, he had to start taking over some of Nanna's responsibilities now, to prove to the coven, and to himself, that he was up to the job. Starting with the fire. Traditionally, Nanna always put it out, bringing their wiccan festivities to a close.

Happy to start with such a small and manageable task, Mark waited for the last person to leave, then let his magic flow to suffocate the last of the flames. He flexed his fingers, after using so much dark magic earlier this summer, the natural magic was still not sitting as comfortably as it used to. It almost felt like Mark's training was back at the beginning – except this time he was aware how rubbish he was.

Mark called the quarters, to try and settle his mind, and tried again. The magic felt slow and reluctant, but as he concentrated harder, it bent to his will. The embers burnt bright for a few moments, before disappearing into ash.

When Mark and his parents returned to their house, Mark saw two figures lingering in the garden. He could just about make out Nanna and Michelle sitting in the shadows. His heart leapt and his stomach flipped – he didn't know whether he wanted to cheer or throw up. Nanna was finally telling *his cousin* the truth.

Out of respect for their privacy, Mark moved away from the window, and made his way to bed. His actions weren't completely noble – he didn't want to suffer the wrath of Michelle or Nanna, if either of them caught him snooping on the big reveal.

Mark would just have to wait 'til morning to find out how it went.

Chapter Three

Despite it being his day off, Mark woke up at dawn, after less than five hours sleep. He knew that it was pointless staying in bed, he wouldn't get back to sleep this morning – his bloody body clock was already a slave to the milking cows' schedule.

Mark got up, hearing his parents still snoring soundly. There had been plenty of beer and wine involved last night, and he'd noticed how these older people needed a ridiculous amount of sleep. He didn't even need to be quiet as he went downstairs; a herd of elephants wouldn't wake his parents this morning.

In the living room, there was a human-sized lump on the sofa, with a duvet over the top.

"Michelle?" Mark guessed.

The duvet twitched and the corner of a face appeared, a dark-brown eye locked on him.

"You OK?" Mark asked.

The girl gave out a groan, and pushed the duvet aside, so she could sit up. Her brown hair was a wild mess, and there were dark circles around her eyes. Mark wondered if she'd gotten any sleep at all.

Michelle watched him suspiciously. "Did you know?" She croaked.

"Only the last couple of weeks." Mark replied honestly. "How do you feel about it?"

Michelle gave him a withering glare. "How do you think I bloody feel?"

Mark chewed on his lip for a moment. "I think this needs bacon…"

He made his way into the kitchen, and quickly knocked up two plates of fresh bacon, eggs, toast; and some of last night's left-over sausages.

Michelle joined him at the table, picking at the food.

"Is there owt I can do?" Mark asked.

Michelle shook her head, then sighed heavily. "No, I just… need to get out of here today. It's not like I've got many options. My bestie Donna is away in Spain this week. My parents – *adopted parents* –

haven't given two shits since I moved here... I could go to Peter's, but I think that would just add flame to his romantic fantasies... and I'm not giving Robert the satisfaction of crawling back to him..."

"I've got no plans 'til tonight, we can go out to the moors and get away for the day. Maybe hit the river if it gets hot." Mark shrugged.

"You'd do that for me?" Michelle asked, warily.

"Sure."

Michelle grunted, as she stabbed a piece of sausage. "Still not your friend."

~~~~~

It didn't take long to pack food, drink and towels. Michelle had been given Mark's old bike, and they headed along the road, before taking the most direct track into the wilderness.

Mark breathed in the cool morning air. He'd always thought that the Yorkshire Moors were beautiful; but they seemed extra special on a summer's dawn. As they pedalled onto the rolling landscape that hadn't changed for centuries, it quickly felt like they were a million miles away from the rest of the world. There was just Mark, Michelle, and their spirit animals.

Michelle had let her crow loose as soon as they left the house, and Mark quickly followed suit. Luka looked like your everyday border collie and barked as he raced after their bikes.

Mark let Michelle set the pace, and gave her the space she clearly needed, following at a safe distance.

Eventually, Michelle pulled up. Mark was secretly pleased, his legs were burning, and he wasn't sure how much longer he could have kept cycling.

"Y'know, the ironic thing is – I *wanted* to be a part of your family. I kept wishing that Nanna would officially adopt me, and that I would have *good* people in my life. No more secrets, a fresh start." Michelle spat. "It serves me right – I learnt long ago that I shouldn't dream better for myself. But your Nanna roped me in, made me foolish enough to think…"

"I think Nanna only wants what's best…"

"Really? And what part of my shitty life has been the 'best'?" Michelle snapped. "I was only a few miles down the road, but she never once tried to contact me. I've seen you learning about being a witch beside her so naturally; yet I had to learn witchcraft from a damned demon!"

"I'm sorry." Mark said, the words seeming grossly inadequate. He'd been so lucky to have the support of his family, and the freedom to choose to be a witch. He gave a strained smile. "And in further bad news, you're stuck with me now, *cousin*."

The anger faded a little from Michelle's eyes, but she didn't say anything.

"Want to find somewhere to sit and eat?" Mark asked.

"No." Michelle scowled, looking down at the river. "I want to learn how to swim."

"What?"

"You said you'd teach me any time. I don't want to be the freak that can't swim, on top of the black sheep of your weird family." Michelle demanded.

Mark shrugged. "Fine. Swimming it is."

Twenty minutes later, and they were at the best swimming spot of the river, where it ran wide and slow. They'd dropped their bikes onto the bank, and Mark was getting ready to give his first swimming lesson.

He wished he had a younger brother or sister to practise on, before having to teach his volatile cousin, but there was nothing to be done.

"Right, um. We have to get in the water." Mark said hesitantly.

"Well, duh!" Michelle snapped, eyeing the river warily, as if it would jump up and sweep them away.

Mark stepped into the water, the current tugging lazily at his legs. Behind Michelle, he could see her crow spirit huffing and ruffling her feathers restlessly. She probably shared Michelle's agitation, and worse, there was no real threat to protect her from. She cawed and chattered; whilst in contrast, Luka lay relaxed, basking in the sun.

Mark felt Michelle's hand tighten on his arm, as she tip-toed into the river for the first time. "It's friggin' freezin'!"

"Well, duh." Mark echoed. It always seemed to surprise people how cold it was to swim in nature's waterways.

Michelle held her breath, as she walked deeper, the river lapping at her chest.

"We can stop there, if that's enough for one day?" Mark suggested, not wanting to push her too fast. He didn't need to read her aura to feel the sharp fear emanating off her.

"I said I wanted to *swim*, not paddle like a toddler." Michelle snapped. "Stop being such a soft git, and teach me."

"You're welcome." Mark huffed, no longer surprised or upset by Michelle's little outbursts.

"You'd best practise sticking your head under water, so you don't panic when it happens by accident."

Michelle looked at him like he'd asked her to walk over burning coals.

"Just get it over with. Blow slowly through your nose the whole time, to stop water getting up it."

Michelle counted down from three, then ducked under water with such force, she nearly knocked Mark over. Air bubbles blew up and Mark felt Michelle's fear stab acutely.

She panicked and pedalled her arms wildly, trying to find the right way up. The water swirled violently around her…

Mark staggered back out of the way, as an unnatural wave raised up higher than his head, coursing around his cousin and deposited her back on the riverbank. The water broke away from whatever spell held its shape, and Mark heard Luka yelp at the surprise soaking he got.

Trembling on her hands and knees, Michelle coughed out a lungful of water, then glared at Mark. *"What did you do?"*

"That… wasn't me." Mark said numbly, sitting back on his heels and looking at the river.

He closed his eyes, he felt the power of the water, deep and resonant, and moving swiftly back to its natural calm, after the magic had disrupted it. Opening his eyes, Mark looked uncertainly towards Michelle.

"I think it's safe to say that water is your strongest element." Mark mused. "You didn't even need to use a verbal spell…"

"What?"

"Most witches have a natural affinity for one of the four elements. Despite all your irrational fears of it, it looks like water is yours. That was a freakin' powerful spell!"

"Well, I don't know if you've heard, but I come from a long line of powerful witches." Michelle said bitterly, as she gazed at the river.

Tentatively, the girl crawled back to the water's edge, and reached out to it. The river responded to her proximity, drawing up to her hand, and rippling underneath like a pet cat demanding attention.

"Huh."

Mark could feel the fear wash away from his cousin, as she embraced this part of her magical identity. Mark only hoped she would accept her part in his family as quickly.

Michelle got to her feet, and stepped back into the river, this time, her eyes were bright with curiosity, instead of dread.

"What's your best element?" She asked, her hands playing with the currents of the river.

"Dunno." Mark shrugged. He recalled the horse he'd summoned in the demon realm, all fire and stone. Robert – the fire demon – had seemed intrigued by his creation; Mark feared to have anything in common with him, even as he enjoyed the feeling of controlling those flames.

They stayed by the river for a couple of hours, until Michelle could do an acceptable doggy paddle. She quickly got the hang of treading water, and clearly enjoyed floating along the surface. Mark had never seen her at such peace before.

He kept an eye on her, but couldn't help trying his own magic. It was such a relief that it felt natural and normal once more. Mark couldn't believe how much it had freaked him out when it clashed with the lingering shadow of dark magic. He'd missed how the natural magic sang to him, in every blade of grass, the strength of the earth around him resonating with power. Mark couldn't help but call up a fire, trying to shape it into something vaguely horse-shaped. Struggling to sustain it, the best he could manage was a wonky Shetland pony.

Mark sighed, and let the spell fall away. He noticed Michelle watching him with a smug expression.

"Are you coming to Harry's gig tonight?" Mark felt a red blush heat his neck and tried to shift the focus.

Michelle chewed on her lip for a minute, then shook her head. "No, I'm not ready to play happy families yet. And I can't stomach bein' stuck in a car with *her*."

Chapter Four

The sun was still shining when they got to the club at York that evening.

It was the first time Mark had physically seen posters declaring that Not-Dave was playing, and it all seemed surreal. Harry seemed to take it all in his stride, casually walking past. His façade lasted a minute, before he grinned like an idiot, running back to the poster, so Sarah could take photos for his Instagram.

Harry was on at nine – a good time, Sarah announced – late enough to be busy; and early enough for most punters to be sober. It was good to get paid for gigs, but Sarah insisted that they had to look at the bigger picture – Harry growing his fanbase.

Mark walked into the biggest venue his friend had played to date. The old hall had two levels, and both of them were already heaving.

A band was currently onstage, their music flowing out over the crowd.

"Oh my god! You're Not-Dave!" A couple of girls popped up; a few years older than them. The speaker blushed red, but her eyes were sparkling. "I follow you on Instagram, I totally love your voice."

"Um, thanks." Harry said, a little startled.

"Can we have a selfie?"

"Um, sure?" Harry glanced over to Sarah, waiting for her to object.

Instead, his manager-slash-girlfriend offered to take the photo.

Harry shot Mark an amused look, before beaming towards the camera phone.

"Thank you." The girl trilled, as she took back her mobile. "Is there anywhere we can buy your music? I can't find it online."

"No." Harry replied with a sorry shrug.

"*Not yet*." Sarah corrected. "We've got a studio booked soon, so it should hopefully be shortly after that."

"Oh, excellent, we'll watch out for it. Thanks, Not-Dave." The girl rushed away, glued to her phone screen.

"Hey, can I have a selfie, too?" Mark teased.

"Shut up." Harry punched his arm to hide his embarrassment.

"Recording in a studio – that's exciting news!"

"Yeah, my manager thought it was the natural next step." Harry chewed his lip. "Will you… come with?"

"Yeah, of course I'll be there!" Mark grinned.

Mark checked his phone again. Damian was supposed to meet him here, with his Aunt Maggie and Miriam, but the trio were late. Mark chewed his lip, as his call to Damian's phone went straight through to voicemail. He didn't *want* to be paranoid, but the last time he couldn't contact his boyfriend was because he'd been kidnapped by demons and locked in a demonic prison.

Mark hung up and scrolled through his contacts until he found Miriam's number. His finger hovered over the screen, wondering if he should be pestering his covenmate, before he finally hit call.

It rang a few times, before it was finally picked up.

"Hello?" Miriam answered warily.

"Hey Miriam, it's Mark. Just checking you're all OK. Damian didn't answer his phone." Mark rushed to explain.

"We're fine." Miriam said slowly. "Why?"

"Well, you're not at the venue yet…"

"Shit." Miriam swore.

Mark could hear a muffled conversation between two women.

"Sorry Mark, we forgot we'd made plans tonight." Miriam came back on the phone. "We got the chance to visit Scarborough for the weekend… Can you please apologise to Harry for us?"

"Yeah, will do." Mark said. "So, Damian's alright?"

"Yeah, when we left him this afternoon, he was on his PlayStation. Chances are, he wouldn't notice a bomb dropping, never mind his phone."

Mark felt a little better about his boyfriend. Short of abandoning his best friend's gig, and getting the bus home, there was nothing he could do. Mark couldn't wait 'til he was seventeen, and could drive himself, instead of relying on public transport, which in the countryside was sparse at best.

Getting a bus to Tealford, then one to Damian's village would take over two hours. He figured it was almost quicker to stay for the gig and get a lift back with his family.

When Mark went back into the main room, the band had been replaced by a single figure, standing on stage, cradling the microphone. They may have been on their own, but they had a haunting and powerful voice; their aura filling the stage.

The audience hadn't been particularly rowdy, but everyone's conversations were put on hold; as they were mesmerised by the singer.

Mark looked up at the stage, wondering who was weaving such musical magic. He didn't recognise them, a normal-looking young person, with black hair hanging loose around their face, a dark green top and black jeans were understated, but very stylish.

Mark popped up next to Harry, whose eyes were locked on the latest performer.

"Where's Damian?" Harry asked, not looking away from the stage.

"Not coming. His adults forgot." Mark sighed. "Miriam said sorry."

"Uh-huh."

Mark returned his gaze to the stage. "They're good."

"Uh-huh." Harry repeated.

The singer finished their set and was replaced by a couple of guys with a keyboard and guitar. The new duo's upbeat music faltered a little, in the aftermath of the last singer; but they eventually found their rhythm.

The hypnotic spell lifted from the crowd, and they began to chatter enthusiastically once more.

The mystery singer appeared at the stage door and made a beeline for Harry and his friends.

"Good set." Harry said in greeting.

"Thanks, I told you it would be." They had a gentle Scottish lilt to their voice, and Mark didn't know if their confident statement was dry humour, or real arrogance.

"This is Coira – they moved to Yorkshire recently." Harry introduced. "Coira, this is Mark; and you already know Sarah."

"Oh, cool. Are you going to college in September?" Mark asked, not quite sure how old Coira was.

They looked at Mark with startlingly-green eyes weighing him up, before eventually replying. "Yes, I'm signed up to Tealford College."

"Oh great, us too. At least you'll know a few fellow students before you start." Mark paused.

"Um, not that I'm saying you need our help to make friends… or that you want to be friends with us…"

Coira tilted their head at his rambling. "Thanks."

"Coira played some of the same gigs as me this month. They were, er… a bit rough." Harry said, looking a little guilty at his assessment.

"I told you, I was out of practise." Coira smiled at his discomfort.

"By out-of-practise, you mean 'crap'." Harry teased.

Mark waited for the customary punch from Sarah, whenever her boyfriend put his foot in it; but the blonde girl seemed quite happy to let his mouth run away tonight.

"I gotta go get ready for my set. Are you gonna stay for it?" Harry asked.

Coira gave a slow nod; but when Harry disappeared, so did they.

~~~~~

In anticipation of a late night on Saturday, Mark had cleared Sunday morning off with Mr Brown.

Despite the opportunity for a much-needed lie-in, Mark was out of the house bright and early. Damian still hadn't replied to his messages, and

Mark was anxious to see his boyfriend was safe, with his own eyes.

He cycled the familiar route to the cottage Damian's Aunt owned. It had suffered demon-fuelled fire damage only a few weeks earlier, but there were no signs left outside. The roof had been repaired; only the rooms inside were partly unfinished.

Mark raised his hand to knock, but the door swung open beneath his fist.

"Damian?" Mark called, his worry sparking anew.

He paused, summoning his protective spirit Luka, who looked intently into the cottage with his sheepdog stare.

Mark let himself into the familiar, narrow hallway. He could hear muffled voices and followed them upstairs.

"Damian?" Mark shouted, pulling his magic about him in a defensive spell.

The bedroom door was yanked open by Mark's very naked boyfriend.

"Do you mind? You're ruining the mood."

"Robert!" Mark covered his eyes and turned away, blushing. "What are you doing?"

"Well, I thought that was obvious… I've been stuck at that stupid football camp my host signed up to for a week; it was so drearily dull, I let Damian keep control the whole time. We got back the other day, and I had to blow off some steam."

Mark heard laughter come from his boyfriend's bedroom.

"Who've you got in there?" Mark demanded.

"Wouldn't you like to know." Robert teased. "Don't worry, it's not your new bosom-buddy Michelle."

"I couldn't care less who you're fooling around with." Mark insisted, a hot flush creeping up his neck. "But what if Maggie came home?"

"Miriam whisked Maggie away for a couple of days." Robert shrugged. "Those two are so sickeningly loved up, I don't think they'd notice if they *were* in the cottage."

Mark peeked beneath his fingers, and his blush intensified. "Can you please put some clothes on?"

"Why? I'm sure it's nothing you haven't seen before…" Robert smirked at his discomfort. "Wait… you have seen it before?"

"Not that it's your friggin' business, but Damian and I are waiting 'til it's right." Mark said, embarrassment making him stumble over his words.

"Well, isn't that precious." Robert muttered, grabbing a towel from the radiator with a sharp snap. "I admire your resolve, when your boyfriend's body is as hot as this… although he is a bit of a cold fish, personality-wise. I suppose they cancel each other out."

"*Maybe* our relationship has been bumpy because Damian is being possessed by a psycho demon." Mark argued.

"Psycho? I think that's a little wide from the mark." Robert sounded offended. "What have I ever done wrong?"

"Seriously? You constantly threaten everyone in your path." Mark said.

"*Threaten*." Robert echoed, "I never really hurt them… or at least not in any lasting way."

"*Not lasting*…? What about Damian's parents?"

"His father was bound by oath; once he broke it, there was nothing anyone could do to save him." Robert shrugged. "His mother was collateral damage. If she hadn't been in the car, she'd still be around. Once a curse is set, there's no way to control how it acts."

"And what about Damian's grandmother? His best friend still in a coma? Were they collateral damage too?"

Robert paused, speechless.

Mark risked peeking through his fingers, frowning at the demon's expression. "You forgot about them, didn't you?"

"Human lives are so brief and fleeting. Ten years, twenty, a hundred – it's all over in the blink of an eye." Robert said dismissively. "It's sometimes hard to keep track of all the insignificant ones."

"Insignificant?" Mark repeated. No one should be considered insignificant. "What about me, am I dispensable too?"

Robert looked at him with his ancient black eyes. "No." He replied quietly.

Unable to hold his intense gaze for long, Mark turned away. He took a deep breath, trying to calm his pulse after the argument. Mark never knew where he stood with Robert, trying to speak to him like he was another human being was pointless.

"I like it when you get worked up… if you want to throw me against a wall like you did in London…"

"*Robert!*" Mark snapped, not wanting to think about the passionate kiss he shared with Robert, when he mistook him for Damian.

"One day you'll admit that you want to kiss me…" Robert smirked. "But as you're still too scared to see your real feelings, I suppose I can do something... nice... in the meantime. I'll wake your beau's friend from her coma."

"Really?" Mark asked, wary about what he might want in return. "I won't-"

"There will be no deal necessary." Robert said, raising his hand. "I got what I wanted; having the Lykaois girl in a coma serves no further purpose."

"Thanks." Mark replied drily. Even when Robert was playing 'nice', he sounded like he was conspiring for selfish needs.

Chapter Five

Mark didn't know how or when he learned that a kid had gone missing from Tealford. It was a piece of awful news that everyone in town and the surrounding villages just immediately knew.

The community was small and close-knit enough that they were shook when it was announced six-year-old Laura Davies had gone missing. The police had nothing to go on. One minute she had been playing on the public park. The next she had vanished.

Her picture was all over social media, and the police were out in force, combing the area. Her parents left paralysed with the gut-wrenching knowledge that their baby girl was beyond their protection.

The day after little Laura went missing, the police showed up at Nanna's kitchen door.

Mark looked up from his book on herblore. He recognised the policeman as part of the coven. It wasn't unusual for the police to visit, in the hope that Nanna could help find someone they were looking for.

This was the first time it was for a missing child.

The officer nervously twisted a blue jumper in his hands, the shiny unicorn motif looking inappropriately cheerful. "I thought we could... scry from this..."

"Of course, Will. Come on in."

"I was gonna pick up Denise on the way to form the circle... but she's got so much on her plate with Danny, I didn't want to bother her." Will made an awkward gesture towards Mark. "Will he be able to help?"

"Yes, although it's better with four..." Nanna replied, volunteering Mark for the job. "Mark, can you grab Michelle? If she'll come?"

Mark closed his book and pushed away from the kitchen table. Despite living in the same house, Mark didn't think Michelle had spoken a word to

Nanna since the big reveal. This was the perfect chance for Nanna to get her talking again – dangling some magic as temptation.

Mark headed up to the spare room and knocked. There was no reply, but he could hear Michelle's music playing.

"It's only me." He called.

As if by magic, the door opened, his cousin hovering behind it. Her once-open-hostility was now replaced with mild-suspicion. "What?"

"We've got spellwork to do." Mark said, stepping into the small room.

Tigger the cat curled up in his new-favourite place on Michelle's bed. The window was open, and Mark could spy Michelle's crow perching on the tree outside.

"Y'know, you're free to go into the garden anytime you want." He remarked.

"I don't want to be the presumptuous lodger. It's not just Nanna's garden, it's your parents too." Michelle blushed and turned away.

"Don't be daft – you're a permanent part of the house. And… you're family." Mark shrugged.

"Yeah, but that don't make it any less awkward when your mum's doing yoga. Having me hovering about can't be relaxing."

"If you spoke to her about it, she'd probably ask you to join her. She tried to get me into it, but it wasn't my thing..." Mark gave a sigh. "Anyways, back to business. The police want to scry for that missing girl. Nanna asked if you wanted to be part of the circle, but if you'd rather sulk up here..."

Michelle narrowed her eyes, weighing up the pros and cons. Then pushed past Mark. "You are *so* transparent. What are you waiting for, loser?"

Mark followed Michelle downstairs. She didn't say a word to Nanna or the waiting policeman, just gave them a death glare and marched outside.

The officer looked bemused by her reaction. "Isn't that the girl who stole the chief's car?"

"*Borrowed*." Mark said in her defence. He was about to say that Michelle hadn't stolen a vehicle in ages, but the words died in his throat. It was only last month they had 'borrowed' Nanna's Landrover, when they needed to visit a local dark coven.

"Huh." The officer didn't look convinced.

"Michelle is an excellent witch, and... my granddaughter. She is very capable of helping us today." Nanna said in a no-nonsense voice.

The policeman didn't look any happier, but took a deep breath and followed the moody teenager outside.

Nanna went to move, but Mark stopped her.

"Are you sure this is a good idea? Last time we did a location spell it knocked you out. We can get another witch to join." Mark said, thinking back to last month, when he'd needed Nanna's help to find Damian. Mark had been terrified to see his super-strong Nanna crumple into something grey and lifeless.

Mark thought he saw Nanna's usual bravado waver.

"I may be stepping down soon, but I still have responsibilities. There is a missing child, and I... can't... not help." Nanna argued. "I have been the Grand High Witch for thirty years, and if there is anything I can do to help, I will. If I don't, and something happens to the girl, it will be on my conscience."

Mark sighed, he knew from a lifetime's experience, that arguing with Nanna was pointless. "Fine, but I'm taking the lead on the spell. And you're going to play a passive role in the circle."

"But-"

"No 'buts'. Me and Michelle can do the hard work. I think between the two of us, we're nearly as powerful as you, oh 'Grand Highness'." Mark crossed his arms. "Remember, I get my stubborn streak from you, so you have no chance of changing my mind."

Mark walked out into the garden, to see the policeman and the ex-ASBO-girl standing in awkward silence.

"Let's get started." Nanna stated, waving them into place, and moving quietly to the south point.

A shiver ran up Mark's spine as he silently stepped into the north point of the circle that she had ceded. It typically represented earth – Mark had always felt more of a connection to the element of fire, but he now felt something resonate deep within him. Perhaps it was just the Grand High magic recognising him as the official heir.

Out of curiosity, he inspected the witches around him. The policeman was stood to his left, and was easily the weakest witch that Mark had ever worked with; but it didn't seem to matter. The grey lull was soon filled with power, and Mark heard the officer gasp as the first wave of magic washed against him.

Nanna was obeying him so far. Her power was a furnace, and she kept it wrapped tight about her; reflecting the group's magic, but providing none of her own.

This was the first time he'd allowed himself to look at Michelle's magic. She had embraced her affinity for water, and she practically glowed. It was hard to believe this was the same twisted little dark witch that had plagued them. Mark could see there was still a well of untapped power, and he was suddenly glad that Michelle was now on their side.

"C'mon loser. Stop the nebbing, and start the spell." Michelle broke into his thoughts.

Mark flushed red, embarrassed to be caught out. He took hold of the kid's jumper and started to chant the location spell. The others followed his lead, and Mark felt the magic swell, and shape itself to their will. The cloud turned grey, and darkened, showing nothingness.

"What does that mean? Did the spell not work?" The policeman asked, his voice wavering.

"It worked. The girl is somewhere dark." Nanna replied quietly. "Mark, you need to look closer for clues."

Not quite sure what else to do, Mark followed his instincts, and let his consciousness dive into the spell. The darkness surrounded him, and he no longer felt the summer sun on his back. It was cold, and damp; the sound of water dripping with a distinct echo.

"Where is she?" Nanna asked, her voice pulling him back to reality.

Mark blinked in the bright sunlight, and let the spell dissipate, before it could exhaust his Nanna again.

"I don't know. A cave? There was water nearby." Mark took a deep breath to steady the rush of adrenaline from the spellwork. "I think... I could taste salt on the air, I think it was seawater?"

"I thought these spells gave an exact location..." The officer said, the disappointment clear in his voice.

He looked briefly in Mark's direction, and Mark could guess his thoughts – if Nanna had led the spellcasting, he'd have a grid reference and could set off with the blues and twos immediately.

"Not always." Nanna replied coolly. "In my experience, this means someone is deliberately using magic to hide their location. It could be a demon, witches; or even a regular human using a witch's spell or amulet."

Mark noticed Nanna's subtle glance in his direction when she said 'demon'. Silvaticus was under house-arrest; and Robert was on his best behaviour – was another demon in the area? Taking advantage of their absence?

"Get your people to search the coastlines." Nanna ordered, very much in her Grand High Witch role. She snatched the kid's jumper out of Mark's hands and thrust it back at the policeman. "I'll contact the covens, drum up some more manpower."

The officer took his cue and left immediately.

"Do you really think a demon is interfering?" Mark asked, watching the police car pull down the drive.

"What?" Nanna was looking decidedly pale but was at least steady on her feet this time. "Oh... maybe. It could be dark witches; we've got enough of them gunning for us."

"Oh." Mark was so preoccupied with demons these days; he'd forgotten about Edith and her cronies.

"Or it could be a complete unknown. A normal human could have bought the block from a witch. A wise move, as it was inevitable we'd get involved."

"Alright, what's next?"

"Next is a cup of tea, then I'll contact the witches." Nanna said with a sigh.

Mark could feel the fatigue rolling off her. "Uh, no. Michelle can put the kettle on, and I can do the contacting. Do you have a phonebook?"

"Bah, phonebook? Get with the times, lad. There's a WhatsApp group. I'll add you to it."

Mark shared a bemused look with Michelle, and ushered Nanna back towards the kitchen.

Chapter Six

The day of Harry's first recording arrived, and Mark met them at the train station, to travel to the studio in Harrogate.

He kept glancing towards the platform entrance, waiting for Damian to appear. The train was due any minute, and his boyfriend was cutting it very close.

'*Are you still coming?*' Mark's message sat, still unread.

"Perhaps he's stuck in traffic." Sarah offered. "Or his Aunt forgot again? She does seem the type."

"Yeah." Mark replied, looking from the gateway to the big digital board that declared the train was imminent. Mark sighed and tried to call Damian, but it just went through to voicemail.

The train appeared, and he hung up.

"Do you want to… we can wait…" Harry offered.

"No, don't be daft. We're not gonna be late for the studio." Mark said, grabbing his arm and dragging his best friend on the train, before he could argue. "We've gotta pretend to be professional and punctual… at least until you become big enough to do what you want!"

"Yeah, 'cos that's totally my style." Harry snorted.

Mark smiled dutifully, but was distracted. This was the second time in two weeks that Damian had stood him up without warning. The first time was Robert's fault. Mark remembered all his fears that had turned out to be unnecessary. He slowly turned his phone in his hands – was he always going to fear the worst every time his boyfriend was out of touch?

Mark tapped out a message to Miriam, '*Is Damian OK? He's missed our trip. Not answering his phone.*'

A few minutes later, Mark's phone started to ring, and Miriam's name flashed up on the screen.

"Hey, what's happening?" Mark asked, jumping straight to the point.

"We're in London." Miriam replied.

"What? That's not safe, why-"

"Damian got a call this morning from an old friend…" Miriam paused. "Konnie Lykaois is awake."

"Who…? Wait, Damian's best friend is out of her coma?"

"Yes, she woke up a few days ago. We're at the hospital now."

Mark felt uneasy. They'd willing gone into dark-witch territory, to see a victim of demon magic. "You'll be careful."

"Always." Miriam promised. "We'll keep under Edith's radar."

"Alright. Make sure you call me if you need any help."

There was a prolonged pause, and Mark could just picture Miriam's expression at the help from the teenage witch.

"Thanks." She eventually said.

"I meant please call me – not Nanna - she doesn't need the stress." Mark explained.

"Alright." Miriam sighed. "But only if you promise not to do anything stupid."

It was Mark's turn to pause, and Miriam chuckled on the other end of the line.

"I'll get Damian to give you a call later. Bye."

Mark stared at his phone after the call ended. Was this a result of his talk with Robert? Had the demon followed through on his promise to release the cursed girl? Or was it part of a bigger plan; a trap that Mark couldn't see?

"So, what's the story?" Harry prompted, when Mark joined them at their seats.

"You remember Damian's best friend ended up in a coma last year... she's awake." Mark said. "Damian and his adults are down in London to visit."

Harry and Sarah sat in shock, until eventually Sarah spoke. "Isn't that... the same family who tried to poison us? In some weird debt to Edith?"

"Yeah." Mark said, paling at the memory of how close they came. "Technically, Mrs Lykaois did poison you two; you just didn't have any magic to block."

"Do you wanna... it wouldn't take much to switch to the London train at the next station." Harry offered quietly.

Mark was moved that his friend would be willing to drop everything; and go on another potentially dangerous trip.

"No, this is your first trip to a studio. You've been dreaming of this for ages." Mark shoved his phone back in his pocket. "Miriam will call if they need the cavalry."

*****

The studio was a nondescript-looking place on one of the smaller streets in Harrogate. Mark and Harry were both awestruck as they stepped inside; but Sarah moved confidently, chatting with the sound engineer she'd hired, confirming all the details of today's session.

"Wow, it's really happening…" Mark grinned, as they got the tour of the studio, and mixing desk.

Harry grinned back, uncharacteristically quiet.

"Let's get started." The engineer announced, pointing Harry towards the other side of the glass. "We'll begin with a sound-check."

Harry proceeded to play his guitar, then sing a portion of one song, before breaking off sharply. It seemed to take an age to get the perfect levels; but eventually the engineer gave the go-ahead to start working on the beds.

Harry played his guitar, starting at the beginning of his first song, but got stopped thirty seconds in.

The engineer gave him some feedback; Harry nodded and started again. This time, he got a full minute in, before stopping and having to start again.

Mark was surprised at the whole stop-start process. It was hard to stay focussed, and his attention kept drifting to his phone, checking for messages. Mark had thought they'd get through the whole album today; but by the end of the two-hour session, they'd only recorded a single song.

"That's about standard. The engineer is familiar with Harry's sound now, so next time will be a bit faster." Sarah checked her phone. "I need to confirm the next meeting. I'll be back in a tick."

Mark watched Sarah head back into the studio and turned to Harry. "You must be thrilled. You're like, a proper recorded artist now!"

"Well, I will be when the album is finished." Harry replied with a strained smile.

Mark knew his best-friend so very well, and he couldn't understand why he wasn't more excited to have his dreams come true. "But?"

Harry glanced back at the studio, to make sure Sarah wouldn't overhear him. "It's what I've always wanted, but it's not how I imagined."

"What do you mean?"

"I love performing live, and… I don't want to sound arrogant; but I thought I sounded alright." Harry glanced again at the studio. "This is… flat. It's not the same… and I feel guilty 'cos Sarah's put so much effort into it."

"Well, isn't that normal? The Artic Monkeys gigs we've been to are so much more alive than their albums."

"Hmph." Harry grunted, not entirely convinced.

Chapter Seven

"I saw Derek at the market today." Mark's Mum said pointedly, as she put down her shopping bag in the kitchen. When Nanna didn't reply, she tried again. "He asked after you."

Mark's attention was peaked, as he recalled the cold non-greeting Nanna had given her hot-farrier-boyfriend at the Summer Solstice.

"Huh." Nanna grunted and busied herself with the salad for tonight's dinner.

Mark rolled his eyes, "What did he do to upset you?"

"Nowt." Nanna replied shortly.

Mark and his Mum shared a look.

"Nanna... what happened between you guys –
it was going so well?" Mum pressed.

"Nowt..." Nanna got out a knife and sliced the
tomatoes with gusto.

"I suppose we could always ask Derek..." Mark
prodded.

Nanna sighed, her hand tightening on the knife.
"I've... noticed his aura changing... he's falling in
love with me."

"Well, that means he has good taste." Mark said
helpfully.

"Of course he has good taste; I'm the epitome of
charm." Nanna snapped.

"Oh, wow, that's...!" Mum smiled at the news,
but it quickly faltered. "Why do I get the feeling that
you're not excited to have a hot guy in love with
you?"

Nanna chewed her lip. "It was supposed to be a
summer fling. It was *supposed* to be flung by now!"

"I don't get it, I thought you liked him?" Mark
asked, frowning.

"I do like him..." Nanna confirmed.

"So... what's the problem?"

"It was always going to be temporary. He was
only going to be here for a few weeks, covering for
his nephew, but... Derek has changed his plans."

Nanna took a deep breath. "He wants to stay a while longer, maybe make a life for himself up here."

Mark had never seen his Nanna look so rattled. "Isn't that a good thing? You guys can spend more time together."

"No. I'm not good for him, not in the long-term. Whilst it was temporary, what we had was perfect. I want to leave it at that." Nanna was fiddling with the salad, refusing to meet their concerned looks. "I can't... drag him into my life. My health is only going to deteriorate. I feel bad enough dragging you lot through it. I can't let someone like Derek get involved... he's a nice guy, he'll feel obligated to stay with me through thick and thin – thin and thin, more like it!"

"Oh, Nanna." Mark's Mum crooned, moving to wrap Nanna in a warm hug.

Nanna gave her an awkward pat in return. "It's all for the best..."

"Does Derek get a say in this?" Mark asked.

"Mark." His mum warned with a sharp glance.

"What? I think it's only fair if he knows all the facts. If you love him, tell him the truth."

Nanna's silence spoke volumes.

"You once told us to stop tiptoeing around like you're already on your deathbed. Well, now it's your turn. You are not on your deathbed, so stop acting like it. Don't use it as an excuse to push away someone you care about."

"Wise words, kiddo. You're really getting the hang of the 'tough love' thing." Nanna chewed her lip. "Fine, I'll speak with him."

"Good." Mark smiled, feeling very pleased with himself.

"That will stop him from looking like a kicked puppy." His Mum added.

*****

Mark decided to get away from the house for a bit that evening. Despite declaring that she agreed with Mark, Nanna was in a mood after his pointed comments.

The warm glowing feeling Mark had after helping soon dissipated, as Nanna started to nit-pick everything.

Damian was still away in London, so Mark couldn't find sanctuary at his; and Harry was at another recording session.

Mark didn't mind being alone, though. He got his bike out and took the track up towards the moors. Mark stopped to call on Luka. Thanks to Michelle's influence, it was becoming habit to let his spirit roam free, even when he didn't need protection.

Just the sight of him helped calm whatever nerves or anxiety he might be feeling.

Mark did wonder what would happen to Luka when he inherited the Grand High Witch powers. Nanna has previously said that she was unable to summon a protective spirit, because she was too powerful. Mark had a sinking suspicion that Luka would leave him forever, which was painful to even think about. He might not be a real dog, but Mark loved him like he was part of the family.

He hadn't voiced any of these suspicions, as he didn't want them confirmed. He was happy to continue in naïve ignorance for just a bit longer.

Mark rode up past the last farms, and out onto the rolling hills. The grey green grass swayed in the breeze, rippling like water in the distance. It felt like he was a million miles from anyone, and any possible problems.

When Mark finally stopped for a break, he stood marvelling over the world below him, feeling free.

Without anyone to judge him, Mark called his magic, which curled around his hands in readiness. He thought again of the fiery horse he'd conjured in the demon realm. He might have been fuelled by dark magic; but Mark saw it as proof of what he could really do.

He'd also seen how powerful Michelle had been, once she had embraced water as her strongest element.

Maybe that's what Mark needed to do. He needed to put aside all his fears. He needed to stop worrying what people would think of him spending time with the flashiest and most destructive magic; and stop worrying that Robert was a fire demon. He was subconsciously crippling himself before he even started.

Mark closed his eyes, and focussed on calling the fire element to his control. It was bright, and leapt eagerly to do his bidding. Mark felt the pure joy as the flame zigged and zagged.

When he opened his eyes, he frowned at the creature he'd created. It was vaguely horse-shaped, in that it had four legs. But it looked like a primary schooler had drawn it.

The creature itself was merely an image, stamped into the world; no more likely to take life, than a scribbling in a book.

Mark sighed, and cracked his knuckles. The creature turned to ash, and gently blew away on the breeze.

Maybe he was going too fast. But it was hard not to, the fire was pure fuel and demanded speed. It felt only natural to cast his spell quickly.

Mark bit his lip, and forced himself to go slower, regardless of the fire magic that danced and begged for him to join in.

He kept a firm hold of his mental image, trying to imprint it in reality. He started at the hooves, and wove the fire tightly into four strong, straight legs. He then focussed on the athletic body, and fine head.

When he was finished, he was sweating from the exertion. Mark stepped back and smiled; it looked just like his Nanna's horse, Lulu.

He reached up to stroke the horse, the fire was hot, but it didn't burn its maker.

Mark's smile faltered, as his hand passed straight through. It was just another insubstantial image. The fire might be real; but the creature wasn't alive, and it looked like Mark's dream of riding was still a long way off.

He tried to tell himself that he'd made a lot of progress today, but it was hard to see a positive in the overall fail.

Maybe he just needed to practise. Maybe he was missing something vital. Or maybe he was just being a fool, thinking he could do it outside of the demon realm, and no dark magic.

Mark stopped fuelling the spell. The burning flames faded, and turned to ash in the air, floating away, to leave no sign of his magic, except for the burnt patches of grass.

Mark ruffled Luka's ears, and the dog looked up at him patiently.

"I'll get there, boy. I'll get there."

Chapter Eight

Mark and Damian sat in the living room of Damian's cottage, playing FIFA on the PlayStation. Normally, Damian would be wiping the floor with Mark; but today he seemed distracted, letting Mark win by his own merit for once, instead of the pity wins.

Mark wondered if the cause was Damian's phone, which kept blowing up with message alerts.

Mark watched as his boyfriend tried to subtly get rid of them.

"Is everything alright?" Mark asked, wondering if he should be jealous of whoever Damian was messaging. "Is it Konnie?"

"Um, some of it. She's coming up to visit." Damian replied quietly. "They'll be here later this week."

"Oh... that'd be... nice." Mark frowned. He was very interested in meeting Damian's best friend, now that she was out of her coma; but he couldn't forget how her parents had betrayed them.

Damian nodded, and fiddled with his phone, clearly uncomfortable with what secrets he hadn't shared.

"If there's someone – I mean, something else – you can tell me." Mark prompted.

"Umm... I've been scouted. Leeds wants me for their Youth team..." Damian said, blushing bright red.

"Seriously?" Mark laughed. "That's amazing news! Why didn't you tell me sooner?"

Damian shrugged. "I dunno, I was worried... didn't want to get our hopes up before it was official."

"But, wow, *Leeds*. I can't wait to tell Dad, he's a big fan." Mark grinned, thinking how excited his Dad would be to hear that Mark's boyfriend had been selected for his favourite club.

Mark watched the uncertainty linger on Damian's face. "No need to worry, you've earnt this."

The doubt didn't lift, as Damian turned back to the screen, his eyes glazed over and unseeing.

"First Harry, now you..." Mark sighed. "You've both achieved your dreams, but I get the feeling that you're not as over-joyed as you should be. I can't work out why..."

Damian hit the pause button and closed his eyes. "I want to tell you my worries; but I don't want you to think any less of me."

"I could never think less of you." Mark said gently, his hand settling on Damian's trembling one.

Damian took a deep breath, but still refused to look at Mark. "You say I've earnt my place; but what if I haven't?"

"What do you mean?" Mark frowned. "You're the best player on the school team. Ugh, bad example, they're pretty crap. But don't let that make you think any less of yourself. You made them better, and everyone saw that."

"No, not that. Robert."

"Oh."

"I was a good footballer down in London; but I was nothing special. I wasn't even good enough to

80

get scouted for low-level teams." Damian idly traced the shape of Mark's hand in his. "I worry it's no coincidence... since Robert became a part of my life, I've gotten faster and stronger."

"You're so committed to your training; it was inevitable that you'd get fitter and more skilled over time." Mark tried to reason.

"Or... it could be a benefit of the symbiotic relationship that Silvaticus speaks of. I've suspected for a while now... and I think you've noticed, too." Damian looked at him, his blue eyes worried.

Mark was stuck for words. He couldn't deny it. He'd long thought that Robert was affecting Damian in subtle ways. He'd never wanted to bring it up, knowing how much stress his boyfriend already shouldered. "What if... what if we could get rid of him?"

Damian fixed his bright eyes on Mark's, searching for understanding. "Why? Have the witches discovered his name?"

"No." Mark said, clinging to how that was technically true – the rest of the coven didn't know Robert's real name... "But if they did, would you still want to be rid of him?"

There was an awkward pause, that went on a moment too long.

"Of course, I want nothing more than to be rid of him." Damian insisted, his gaze faltering.

Mark sat close to his boyfriend, knowing that he was lying, too.

There was a sharp rap at the door, that made them both jump.

Damian frowned at the unexpected visitor, but got up to dutifully answer the door.

"Damian Foster? Is your aunt in?"

Mark jumped up at the sound of the familiar voice. He peeked down the corridor and could see the same policeman who'd helped with scrying for the missing girl.

"Yes, she's in the garden..." Damian replied, nonplussed.

"That's great. May we come in? We were hoping for an informal chat."

"Um... sure?" Damian replied, hesitantly. He turned back into the cottage. "Aunt Maggie?"

Mark watched Will and his colleague follow Damian into the garden. The only space big enough for several adults to comfortably sit. The policeman gave Mark a brief, serious glance.

Mark turned off the game and hurried after them.

"This is private. Mark, Miriam, perhaps you should give us a few minutes."

Miriam gave a little huff. "As this is an informal visit, you have no authority to keep me out of it. If it is a formal enquiry, I will be present to offer Damian legal advice. Besides, Maggie will share every detail, anyway."

Will frowned, but didn't argue. He looked over to Mark again.

"Um, what she said." He motioned to his new hero, Miriam.

"Fine." Will grumbled. "I'm PC Jones, and we're here to ask Damian about Tyler Smith."

"Tyler?" Damian echoed. "He's one of the kids from footie club…"

"He's missing." Will stated.

"What?!" Damian gasped, freezing to the spot.

"He went missing yesterday. He was last seen at the local playground at 5pm." Will checked his notebook. "We understand that you were close with the boy. The football club said that you were his favourite trainer during footie camp."

Damian nodded numbly, then coughed. "Yes, that's right. He was such a character."

"Has he tried to contact you outside of training."

Damian shook his head. "No, never."

"Have you noticed any unusual behaviour from the kids? Or seen anyone acting suspiciously?"

Damian paused, but shook his head. "I… I can't think of anything."

Will and his colleague tried a few other questions, trying to stir something, anything that would help them. When it became clear that Damian wasn't going to provide useful information, Will sighed.

"Well, if you hear, or remember anything, no matter how small, please contact us." Will withdrew a business card from his pocket and handed it to Damian. "We'll… see ourselves out…"

Maggie pulled her pale-looking nephew into a hug, and Mark took the opportunity to catch Will for a quick word.

"Hey." Mark called, catching his attention.

The policeman stopped getting into his car and turned back to him. "Mark. Do you have anything to add?"

"Another kid has gone missing?"

"Yes." Will narrowed his eyes. "Unfortunately."

"And you think Damian can help?" Mark asked, crossing his arms. "Or do you think he's responsible?"

84

"Mark, you might have some tenuous authority over me in the coven; but this is official police business." Will frowned. "This is an ongoing investigation, and we are following up several leads."

Mark rolled his eyes at the official spiel. "Why are you focussing on Damian?"

"I haven't disclosed his demon-possession to the sergeant. Her belief of witchcraft and magic only stretches so far. But I think that it's too much of a coincidence, and we can't ignore the danger he poses."

"Robert isn't the only demon in the area. Besides, he told me he finds the football training sessions boring; and cedes full-control to Damian at those times." Mark argued.

Will shook his head. "You're being naïve – what has he done to make you believe that?"

Mark bit his tongue, he didn't want to admit that he had the ultimate hold over the demon – what reason did Robert have to mislead him, when Mark had the power to get rid of him permanently. "I just… don't want to jump to conclusions."

Will gave a sigh and handed Mark one of his business cards. "You stick to the witch stuff. Leave the real policework to me and my colleagues."

The officer turned back to his car, before Mark could dig the hole any deeper.

Chapter Nine

The first time Mark met Konnie; the whole gang went bowling for the evening. Mark supposed it gave people something to distract them, so they wouldn't all interrogate the new girl immediately.

Mark was a little surprised to see Harry's singer friend sitting in the booth. They looked more relaxed and approachable than the last time Mark had seen them.

"Hey, I didn't know you were coming." Mark said with what he hoped was a welcoming smile. "Um, Cora, is it?"

"Coy-rah" They corrected, with that lovely Scottish melody. "Harry thought I'd like to see what Tealford has to offer in the way of entertainment."

"Oh yeah, the bowling alley, the cinema, and a few restaurants…" Mark gave a bitter smile. He'd grown up in Tealford; he felt equally fond and bored of his hometown's modest offerings.

"It's no bad." Coira replied, bemused at his response.

"What's it like where you're from?"

"I'm from Falkirk originally, but moved around a bit." Coira tilted their head, considering their words. "Most everywhere's the same, really."

"Have you got any more gigs lined up? I'd love to hear you sing again, last time was… magic."

"Nothing lined up yet." Coira gave a shy smile, "But Harry and I are practising together at the weekend. You're welcome to come."

"Really?" Mark asked, looking over to where Harry and Sarah were typing their names into the game.

"Yeah, we might even collab on something." Harry said, excited at the idea.

His girlfriend-slash-manager gave a brittle smile behind him, which left Mark wondering what Harry had done to upset Sarah now.

He didn't get a chance to investigate any further, as Damian came in with a dark-haired girl walking behind him. Konnie's Mediterranean skin was somewhat pale after her many months trapped in a coma, but she was still very bonny. She had a wary and apprehensive smile, as she was introduced to everyone.

"And this is Mark." Damian said, saving the best for last. He slipped his hand into Mark's.

Konnie's smile faltered, and she bit her lip as she saw the small gesture of affection.

"Konnie, you need to add your name, before Harry puts a juvenile alternative in." Sarah piped up, pulling the girl away. "We're doing solos this round, then we usually do teams. You wanna be on my team, my team always wins…"

"Juvenile alternative ready and waiting." Harry confirmed, grinning at the newcomer. "And Sarah always wins because she gets mardy otherwise."

Konnie gave a somewhat brittle-looking smile.

Out of curiosity, Mark turned his attention to the new girl's aura. A sickly brown hovered about her. She had darkness in her life, and was troubled. Mark gave a sigh, he could almost hear Nanna's words, insisting that he helped another girl with a brown aura last year. He'd eventually been able to help Michelle, but she'd been a source of danger in their lives. He only hoped this one was easier.

Mark started to pull his magic back, when he noticed Sarah, still standing next to Konnie. Sarah always had bright, primary colours, matching her bright personality; but Mark was surprised to see a dull red, glowing with hidden problems.

"Are you alright?" Damian asked, snapping Mark's attention back to the present.

"Yeah… I'll tell you later." Mark glanced at Sarah. They were friends, but were they close enough for him to ask her what was wrong? Or would she consider it a witchy violation of privacy? "Let's play."

He squeezed Damian's hand, and pulled him towards the crowded booth, aware of Konnie's eyes fixed on them.

"So, Konnie, how long are you in Tealford?" Mark asked, as he sat down.

"Not sure. The whole summer? I've kinda got no plans." Konnie answered shortly, turning away to watch the others bowl.

"Have you decided what you're doing for college in September?" Sarah asked the most common question amongst their friends.

"Um, no." Konnie blushed. "I missed most of the last academic year, so I've gotta retake it."

"Oh, I'm sorry, ignore me, I'm being stupid." Sarah replied, mortified at her slip.

"S'fine." Konnie said with a shrug.

"Right, bowling." Mark announced, trying to relieve Konnie of all the attention she was clearly uncomfortable with.

He picked up a ball and threw it down the lane with gusto. Mark had no affinity with sports and struggled with anything that needed coordination. His ball drifted to the side and knocked down a single pin; followed by the laughter and jibes of his friends. He grinned sheepishly; it was kinda nice that some things didn't change.

Mark's second roll earnt him a few more points, along with another surge of friendly insults. He was more than happy to cede the floor to the others.

Mark watched as his friends all scored more, placing him in solid last place. Only Sarah made a strike; and Michelle managed a half-strike, with her ball swerving to hit an awkward pin.

"That's cheating." Mark chided, as she walked back to the booth.

Michelle looked bemused at the others openly cheered her on. "Worth it." She replied, without a hint of remorse for her use of magic.

Mark looked up to see Konnie's gaze locked on them, as her trembling hand tightly grasped a locket around her neck. Mark felt the odd sensation that magic was being used; but he couldn't get a single read on it. When he focussed on the swell of power, his attention slipped away uselessly.

"Mark... what's up?"

Mark jumped at Michelle's voice. "Nowt."

His cousin gave a disbelieving grunt. "Sure, tell your face."

Mark rolled his eyes. "A magical mystery." He murmured.

"There's one person to ask..."

Chapter Ten

When he got home, Mark went straight into Nanna's half of the house.

Michelle pushed past him and headed for the stairs.

"I don't mind if you stay." He offered, not wanting to keep any new secrets.

"Yeah, but I mind." Michelle said, a dark look crossing her face, before she disappeared upstairs.

Mark sighed, wondering how long Michelle could keep up this angst with Nanna. He walked into the sitting room, where Nanna was watching Netflix, hooked after being introduced to it by her granddaughter.

Mark sat on the sofa, and half-watched Sex Education, waiting for the episode to end. A ginger mass climbed into his lap and started to purr. Mark stroked the cat, taking comfort from his settling warmth.

Nanna chuckled away, fully-absorbed in the fictional plot and characters. When it finished, she turned to her grandson. "So, small talk; or straight to what's bothering you?"

"I met Damian's best mate from London, Konnie." Mark said. "I got a weird vibe from her."

"Uh, huh. Need a little bit more than that to go on." Nanna prompted.

"I got the feeling she didn't like me." Mark said quietly, keeping his eyes fixed on Tigger the cat.

"Not everyone is gonna like you, lad. It's inevitable." Nanna tutted. "No one is universally liked, not even someone as charming as myself."

"She had a brown aura; like Michelle used to." Mark argued. "She could be troubled... or just plain trouble..."

"This is the girl that just woke from a coma?" Nanna asked, raising a brow.

"Yes."

"A coma that was instigated by a demon?"

Yes."

"And she woke to find her best friend has left London, and has an unhealthy relationship with said demon?"

"Yes."

Nanna snorted, "And you expect the poor girl to be all sunshine and rainbows?"

Mark sighed; he felt a fool when Nanna put it like that; but a part of him still felt uneasy about the new girl.

"You already know what to do." Nanna said. "Give the girl a chance and see if you can help her heal. Look how far you've come with Michelle."

"Ugh, I've still got scars." Mark grumbled, only half-joking about his volatile cousin. "I thought... I thought she was using magic, but I couldn't get a read on it."

This caught Nanna's attention. "It's not unusual for witches to be defensive around others outside their own coven." She eventually said.

"I didn't get the feeling that she's a real witch." Mark confessed. "Although her parents tried to use that potion on me; maybe they use magic in more subtle ways."

"Hmm, maybe I should meet with her parents, try and judge how much of a danger they are."

Nanna mused. "And it might be worth being on your guard around Konnie."

*****

Mark was asleep, and he knew that he was dreaming.

In his dream, his eyes were open, but it was so dark, it was impossible to see anything around him. He sat on a cold rock, that dug uncomfortably into his legs; and his hands rested on what felt like wet sand.

Mark sighed. He really preferred the dreams where he was stranded on a desert island with Damian.

Cursing his stupid subconscious, Mark felt about blindly. Unable to rely on his eyes, his other senses seemed so much sharper. The smell of salt was so strong, he felt like it was coating his nose and throat. He could hear the sound of water everywhere, dripping off the walls, into shallow pools. Further away, there was the steady rush of waves upon a pebble beach.

He then heard a high-pitched whimpering…

"Hello?" Mark said, his quiet voice reverberating around him. "Is anyone there?"

There was more whimpering, whoever was there sounded young.

"I'm not going to hurt you," He tried to say in a reassuring tone, but the echo corrupted it. "I'm here to help."

He could hear their sniffling breaths, as they moved closer, the pad of footsteps in the dark. It made his skin crawl, being blind to any monster waiting for him in the dark.

Mark jumped when six small, cold hands started to pat him down, as they blindly felt for him.

Six hands… three children… another one had gone missing.

*****

Mark jerked awake. His heart pounding. He ran a hand through his sweaty hair, as he gazed about him. He was back in his bedroom, the darkness was that of night, rather than the pitch-black cave. He could make out everything in shades of grey. His clock glowed showing it was 3am, still an hour before his alarm went off.

He ran over his dream; he'd not had such vivid hallucinations since his visions of Eadric. As always, the thought of Eadric was like a punch to the gut. This time it was worse, it was compounded with the fact that Mark had dreamt a third child was missing.

Mark got out of bed, restless. He went to the window, but there wasn't even a hint of dawn, so it was too early to go to work.

Movement caught Mark's eye, and he looked down. In the field next to the house, a lone shady figure stood. It seemed to sense Mark's attention, and its head turned to face him, a challenge in its dark eyes.

*****

Mark jerked awake again. He pinched his arm to make sure it was really real, then rushed to the window. The mysterious figure was no longer there – if they'd been there at all.

Mark's sleep-deprived brain tried to process what had happened. He knew that what he'd seen was a real, magic-driven vision; and not just a vivid dream. Which meant that a third child was about to go missing, or already was…

Mark hovered in the middle of his room for a few minutes. It was still 3am in the morning. He might make some enemies; he might sound like a madman, but he couldn't risk another kid's safety.

He rummaged through his jeans pockets until he found PC Jones' business card. Mark prayed he was working the night shift and hit call.

"Jones here." Came a very sleepy voice.

Mark silently swore. "Hi, Will, it's Mark. Sorry to bother you, but it's urgent."

"Do you have news on your demon buddy?" Will said, much more alert.

"Not really... I strongly suspect another kid has gone missing."

"What, how?" Will asked.

"Um... I had a vision of the cave. There were definitely three children there." Mark said, a hot blush creeping up his neck at the confession.

The police officer didn't reply immediately. Mark could tell this wasn't the news Will was hoping for.

"A vision, right." Will muttered. "Did you get the name of the victim?"

"No, sorry."

"Did you see what they looked like?"

"No, sorry. It was still pitch-black." Mark replied.

"So, essentially, I've got to go to my captain and tell them you had a *dream* about a missing kid; but no name and no details to go on?" Will said drily.

"It's not like I'm in control of my visions." Mark snapped.

"Y'not makin' this any better." Will said with a sigh. "Talk me through what happened."

Mark grimaced at the thought of trying to persuade the sceptical copper, but obediently repeated every part of his dream, including the jarring dream-within-a-dream element.

"So... you witnessed a suspicious figure... I think I can use that." Will said. "Before I do, can you promise this is a real vision, and not just a vivid dream?"

"I promise."

"If this is a wild goose chase-"

"I swear I'm telling the truth."

There was silence on the other end, and Mark began to wonder if the policeman had hung up.

"Right, boss." Will finally said. "I'll see what I can do."

*****

Mark knew that getting back to sleep would be an impossibility, so he got up and made his way into Nanna's side of the house, so he could speak to her as soon as she woke up.

He was nursing his third cup of coffee, idly stroking the cat curled up on his lap, whilst perusing the thick tome of the *Dictionnaire Infernal*. Mark had half-hoped he'd be inspired and find a demon that was the perfect culprit, but this old-fashioned book with its crazy ramblings was just giving him a buzzing headache. Maybe he should switch to tea for his next drink.

At a little before 8am, Mark's phone vibrated. His heart fell as he checked the message. Will confirmed that a young girl had been reported missing. Imara Begam had gone to bed as normal, and was missing by the time her parents went to wake her up.

"What's up?"

Mark tore his eyes away from the screen to see Nanna hovering at the bottom of the stairs. "Another kid has gone missing."

"Ah."

"I had a vision that there was a third one... I wish I was wrong." Mark said, his fingers curling tight around his mug.

Nanna patted him on the shoulder and made her way to the kettle. "Did you see anything that helps us find them?"

Mark shook his head, but dutifully relayed everything that happened.

Nanna pursed her lips. "In good news, all three kids are still alive."

"Do you have any better idea who's behind this?" Mark asked.

It was Nanna's turn to shake her head. She flicked through her morning emails on her phone, then froze. "We might find out more later. The town council has invited everyone to a meeting this evening."

Chapter Eleven

Tealford Town Hall buzzed with noise and activity, as the locals poured in. The summer evening was warm, but made stifling as they filled the hall.

Mark filed in behind Nanna and his parents. The invitation had said it was for adults only, but his family had given him the choice to come. As it was more important than a dreary petition for new road signs, Mark had jumped at the chance.

Mark saw Mr and Mrs Johnson, but there was no sign of Harry, who must have chosen to stay home. He caught sight of Sarah sitting with her parents, and gave her a wave.

"Good evening, ladies and gentlemen. Thank you for coming on such short notice." The mayor said, stepping out on the wooden stage. "As you all know by now, another child has gone missing. Assistant Chief Constable Bathgate from the North Yorkshire Police is with us tonight and would like to speak to you all."

The mayor gestured to the senior member of police, and stepped backwards, ceding the stage.

ACC Bathgate moved forward. "Thank you, mayor. Imara Begam makes it three children that have vanished under mysterious circumstances. Please rest assured that my officers are doing everything in their power to find these kids. Stopping whoever is responsible is our highest priority." She paused, looking around at the expectant faces. "That being said, we welcome any help from the public. Anyone who has any information, or has seen anything at all, please don't hesitate to contact us. Whatever you have to say will be kept in the strictest confidence-"

"We all know who is behind this." A sharp voice piped up from the seated audience.

The Constable looked taken aback by the interruption and frowned, scanning the crowd for the speaker. "I'm sorry, Miss...?"

"Mrs Woodington." The woman took this as an invitation and stood up, Mark had an uneasy feeling of recognition, but couldn't remember where he'd seen the woman before.

"Mrs Woodington, if there is relative information you wish to share, you are welcome to come down to the station-"

"Witches." She blurted out.

"I beg your pardon?"

"The witches are behind this." Mrs Woodington insisted.

The Constable, not being a resident of Tealford, wasn't sure what to make of this. She frowned in the mayor's direction, looking for support.

"Now, Mrs Woodington." The mayor started. "That is a heavy accusation to make, we have a long history with the witches, they make up an integral part of Tealford. You can't think they're responsible for this."

"They invite darkness and danger. If they are not directly responsible, they are still the cause of this." Mrs Woodington continued, giving a sniff of disgust as she openly looked in the direction of Nanna and her family.

Mark felt his blood rise at the audacity of this woman to publicly blame his coven.

Meanwhile, Nanna was ignoring her, tapping something out on her phone, before looking calmly back at her accuser.

Mark's phone buzzed with a message from Nanna. *'Don't say a word. You'll only dig the hole deeper.'*

Mark rolled his eyes. Was he really so predictable?

"They use *magic*." Mrs Woodington spat the word. "They are completely wild and unregulated. They should stop their practises – see if that stops any further disappearances!"

Mark could see Nanna's magic curl around her hands, ready to be used to defend herself; but she still continued to sit silently.

"Now, Mrs Woodington, I hardly think that's necessary. It's because of the local coven that we have been given a clue as to where the children are being kept." The mayor argued.

"How can you trust them when they may be responsible?" The woman nearly shrieked.

"We are not discussing this further, tonight." The mayor said firmly, crossing her arms. "If you wish to bring a complaint to the council's attention, you may file it officially during office hours. Now, please can we return our attention to ACC Bathgate."

The Constable looked a little lost, but she coughed, and started to speak again. "Thank you, mayor. I realise that tensions are high, and when something terrible like this happens, it's easy to blame those around you. What we need to do is harder. Tealford needs to stand together, you need to support your neighbours, not accuse them. Finding these children will not be easy, but it will be made even more complicated if you spend your time fighting amongst yourselves."

Mrs Woodington pursed her lips, looking ready to spew more hate, but sat reluctantly down.

The Constable nodded. "We will continue to send out search parties, and would like to remind you that you can sign up as a volunteer with your local police station, or here at the town hall. We ask that anyone with CCTV or footage from your Ring doorbell that may help to contact the police. We recommend those without alarms and cameras look at installing them.

"We are also going to be recommend starting a curfew. We have discussed this with the mayor's office, and we believe it would be wise for children to stay indoors from 7pm to 7am."

There was a rise in noise as people spoke against this. With summer in full swing, and the long sunny evenings the perfect time for families to be out and about. The idea of shutting themselves away was hard to stomach.

"You can't..."

The Constable raised her hand to ask for quiet. "No, legally we cannot enforce this. But we strongly recommend taking a few simple precautions, until the culprit is apprehended, and the missing children found."

Mark bit his lip as he listened to the Constable talk. Curfews were all well and good; but hadn't the latest victim been snatched from her bed? The policewoman was giving reasonable advice, but they wouldn't protect against whatever witch or demon was behind this. Maybe he could get Nanna's advice on making some magical protections for the locals. If anyone would want their help after the witches had been so publicly vilified.

Mark risked a glance over at their accuser and was unsurprised to see Mrs Woodington glaring back scathingly. The feeling of familiarity rose again, followed by the frustration of not knowing where he recognised her from.

The Constable wrapped up her talk, and there was a scraping of chairs as everyone rose at once. The noise of chatter returned, a duller tone, in response to the meeting they'd just sat through.

Mark quietly followed his family, shuffling slowly as they stopped to chat with other adults. He finally spied someone his own age, as Sarah passed by. She looked pale, and tired.

"Hey." Sarah said, her usual bounce completely flat.

"Hey." Mark replied, "Crazy meeting."

"Yeah, those poor kids."

Mark waited for her to say something else; close to, he could see her eyes were red. "You alright?"

Sarah shrugged. "It's nowt. Nuthin' compared to what those families are going through."

Mark frowned. "What's wrong?"

"Um, I think me and Harry are breaking up." Sarah said, the words rushing from her mouth.

"What!"

"I love him so much, but I feel like we're drifting apart..." Sarah said quietly, looking guiltily at the milling crowd. "I just... what kind of person am I, to be torn up over a relationship ending, when there are kids' lives at risk?"

"Oh, Sarah..." Mark moved to give her a hug, but she raised a hand to stop him.

"No, don't. If you hug me, I'll fall apart." Sarah whispered.

"Is there anything I *can* do?"

"Turn back time?" Sarah said with a strangled laugh. "Can witches do that?"

"Um, I haven't had that lesson yet."

Sarah sighed. "Then knock some sense into your best mate?"

"Deal." Mark replied, resisting the urge to wrap his arms protectively around his broken friend.

"I'll um, see you later." Sarah said dully, then ducked out to follow her parents.

Chapter Twelve

Mark finished work early the next day, so he could meet Harry during his lunchbreak. He got to the coffee shop just as Harry was leaving the door, a bag of food in hand.

"Hey, perfect timing. A customer's order got messed up, so I've got an extra panini if you want to share." Harry grinned, waving his prize in Mark's face.

"You messed up their order? Doesn't sound like you."

"Nah, I got it spot on. She wanted a cooked panini to go; but didn't realise she'd have to wait for it to... y'know, *cook*." Harry chuckled at his latest ridiculous customer.

At least working with cows, Mark was saved from the daft behaviour of humans. He didn't think telling the story of how Daisy kept stealing Buttercup's food would be quite as entertaining.

"You missed a right 'Karen' at the meeting last night. She was ready to blame the witches for everything, and burn us at the stake." Mark said, with a shake of his head.

Harry tore off some of the sandwich and passed it to Mark. "Really? Mum and dad always make town meetings sound so boring."

"Mm, she totally hijacked the mayor's meeting, spouting her ignorant hatred. And would you believe Nanna was as meek as a mouse throughout!" Mark snorted and accepted the warm food. "I thought I'd see you there."

"Not my scene. I just hung out with Coira for a bit." Harry shrugged. "I'm surprised you went."

Mark knew he had viewed the town meetings as a yawnfest, and knew there was only one reason he'd gone. "I, um… I had a vision another kid went missing and alerted the police."

"Crap, really?" Harry looked concerned. "Are you alright?"

"Yeah." Mark said, think of the mysterious figure looming outside his house. "Yeah... I um, saw Sarah last night. She said you might be breaking up."

Harry raised a brow at the abrupt change in conversation.

"Is it true?"

Harry shrugged.

"What happened?"

"Dunno, nowt. Lots of stuff... I've only got half an hour for lunch." Harry took a bite out of his panini.

"Is it... Coira?" Mark asked warily, it was clear Harry was close to the newest member of their circle of friends.

"No!" Harry replied too quickly, a guilty blush darkening his cheeks. "Not like that, anyway. Coira is different from anyone I've ever known. They get me; they get what I'm going through."

"But what about Sarah? I thought you guys were the perfect power couple, how can you flirt with someone else?"

"Seriously? You're gonna judge me on that?" Harry snorted. "What about Robert? Eadric? I'm surprised Damian hasn't dumped your arse."

"That's not the same." Mark argued weakly. "This is *Sarah* we're talking about."

"She's changed." Harry confessed, uncharacteristically sombre. "She's not like my girlfriend anymore; there's just the manager, with the next job, the next step in our combined career."

"I'm sorry, mate. Is there anything I can do to help?" Mark said, aware how futile his words were.

Harry shook his head. "So, um, did your vision provide any more clues as to who is behind the disappearances?"

"No, I just saw a dark figure. I couldn't make anything useful out."

"And the police have no new leads?"

"Nowt they shared last night." Mark said with a sigh. "D'you…"

"What?"

"Don't you think it's suspicious… these kids go missing, just as Konnie and her parents come up?" Mark voiced the thought that had been plaguing him.

"Why do you say that?"

"Well, Nanna said it could be dark witches, and they're aligned with Edith's lot." Mark explained. "And when we were bowling the other night – I got the sense that Konnie is very troubled."

"Yeah, but… didn't they only rock up after the first ones went missing?" Harry reasoned.

114

"Officially, yes, I suppose."

"I've gotta get back." Harry said, checking his watch. "Maybe it would be worth investigating the Lykaois family a bit more."

*****

Nanna invited the Lykaois family round shortly after.

As one of the most powerful members of the coven, Denise had also been invited. Along with Mark and Michelle, they'd be able to perform a very strong circle, if it was required.

Even though they were negotiating with potentially dark and dangerous witches, Nanna and Denise looked relaxed and completely unconcerned.

Mark wished he had their confidence.

"Hey, how's Danny?" Mark asked, as they all settled around the table in the garden.

"He's alright, ta. Still committed to his self-imprisonment in the garage." Denise cocked her head aside. "I think he's disappointed you haven't gone back to visit him."

Mark raised a brow, his guilt at not seeing Danny for two weeks being overwhelmed by his surprise. "Really? I was under the impression that he didn't like me, and thought me visiting was a pointless exercise?"

"Yeah, it's amazing what boredom will do to a person." Denise said, helping herself to the buns Nanna had baked. "Either that, or the summer holiday blues have kicked in. He has a superiority complex that constantly needs feeding!"

Mark chuckled, understanding Danny's need to 'teach' a bit more. He noticed Michelle giving him another weird look, and he realised that his cousin hadn't properly met the odious Danny yet. "Maybe Michelle should swing round and meet him. He's awesome – totally awesome – you'll love him."

Michelle scowled in his direction but was prevented from retaliating by the arrival of the guests of honour.

Mr and Mrs Lykaois looked just how Mark remembered, perfectly normal people, whom you wouldn't expect to be allied with dark witches. Their hair was still greying, but they seemed to have lost that tired look. This was probably due to finally being able to relax, now that Konnie was no longer in a coma.

Konnie was still pale – paler when standing next to her parents' healthy Mediterranean colouring. She still looked in pain, her emotional turmoil turning her aura an uncomfortable brown.

116

"Sit, sit. Make yourselves comfortable. We've got tea, iced coffee, juice." Nanna directed, playing the overly-friendly matriarch. "You've met my grandson, Mark. This is my granddaughter, Michelle; and my bestie Denise."

"Thank you for inviting us, after everything that happened in London." Mrs Lykaois said, as she made herself comfortable.

"How are you liking Yorkshire?" Denise asked amicably.

"It's a bit different to what we're used to." Mr Lykaois said quietly.

"Oh, but it is so beautiful." Mrs Lykaois added quickly, in case her husband's words were taken the wrong way. "So much nature, so close to hand. I love it."

"I understand you're something of a herbal witch." Nanna remarked.

"Why, yes." Mrs Lykaois beamed, clearly flattered that the Grand High Witch would know anything about her.

"You should visit Denise's gardens, if you get time. They are lovely, and ever so varied." Nanna offered.

"Oh, my-"

"As long as you don't use any of it to poison other people." Nanna stated, with a pleasant smile. She held out a plate of home-made buns. "Won't you try some?"

Mrs Lykaois' expressions dropped as she looked at the offered food, and she glanced at her husband for support.

"We are very sorry for the part we played." Mr Lykaois said apologetically. "We only did it for Konnie."

At the sound of her name, Konnie scowled in the direction of her parents. She muttered something under her breath and refused to look at Nanna or her coven members.

"Really?"

"We were at our wits' end. She'd been in a coma for nearly a year. Medicine couldn't fix it. My small skill with herbs couldn't fix it…" Mrs Lykaois' lip trembled. "I felt like I'd failed as a parent on every level. I would have done anything for Konnie to wake up again. Then a couple of months ago, the dark coven approached us, with a promise to save her, in exchange for a little help."

"Don't make it sound like you were doin' bleeding laundry for them!" Nanna snapped. "You purposefully poisoned three innocent teenagers and intended to send them powerless into Edith's clutches. It's only sheer luck that Mark managed to avoid it."

"Yes, but-"

"Even with that reprieve, we lost one of our number that day. His name was Eadric." Denise added, her eyes filling with the pain of losing her housemate.

"Yes, but-"

"But what?"

Mrs Lykaois paused, her protest not having been developed any further.

"We didn't mean to hurt anyone." Mr Lykaois said calmly.

"Seriously?" Mark snapped, getting to his feet. "What did you *think* would happen?"

Nanna put a hand on his arm to calm him. "Mark."

"Maybe we should leave." Konnie said her first bitter words at the meeting. "You've already formed your opinion of us. Arguing is pointless."

"Your free to stay or go, as you please." Nanna said, with little warmth. "As the head witch in these areas, I want to know what your intentions are."

"We don't answer-"

"Konnie!" Her father cut in. "We're just here to visit Damian. We're planning on staying here for a few weeks. As you can imagine, it's a relief to be able to get away, now we're no longer shackled to Konnie's hospital bedside."

"Let's make one thing very clear." Nanna said, pulling her magic about her until it was thick and tangible.

A wild wind picked up, whipping dark storm clouds at a frightening speed, turning the pleasant summer sky to night. The dark clouds shuddered and thundered, and there was the unmistakable crackle of lightning. Mark felt the air sucked out of his lungs, and he saw the Lykaois family waver and step back, their eyes filling with fear.

"You don't want me as an enemy. You think Edith is powerful? Dangerous? She's nothing compared to me…" Nanna warned. "Now tell me truthfully – and I will know if you're lying – have you had a hand in those disappearing children?"

A chorus of "no" came from the family, as lightning hit the ground not ten feet away.

As quickly as the storm came, it vanished. The sun shone, and confused birds took up their song again.

"In that case, enjoy your time up here." Nanna said with an innocent smile. "I would recommend Betty's Café in York if you have the time."

The members of the Lykaois family looked between one another, momentarily frozen. Then they scarpered.

Mark sighed, the possibility of establishing a friendship with Damian's old bestie was looking increasingly remote.

He frowned, as Nanna sat down, fatigue visibly coursing through her. "You pushed yourself too much. I thought you were just gonna question them?"

"How boring. This way was much more effective in getting to the bottom of things." Nanna said calmy.

"Sure, you're scary. But if you really wanted to frighten them, you should've set Michelle on them!" Mark smiled.

"I take that as a compliment." Michelle's head popped up as she heard her name. She grabbed one of the buns and looked at it suspiciously. "This isn't, um… really poisoned?"

"It's just lavender from the garden." Denise said. "There's nothing malicious about it."

Chapter Thirteen

Despite the efforts of the police, the mayor's office, and the witches combined, two more children went missing a few days later.

Hanna and Zofia Nowak were sisters living in one of the small villages on the outskirts of the Tealford borough. They had been walking the dog with their dad, never out of sight for a moment. No one could work out how they disappeared, but it devastated the tight-knit community. No one could understand how it could happen in the middle of the day, with witnesses seeing nothing.

The mayor's response was to organise a vigil, to help the people come together and find support with their neighbours. As they gathered in the large town park, their fears and hopes were palpable in the air.

Mark hovered near Harry and Michelle; they were all dressed formally in dark shades. Which Mark now worried looked like they were at a funeral, jumping to the worst possible conclusion.

They stood silently, Mark couldn't think of anything to say. The adults around them seemed to be well-trained at the polite small-talk, exchanging socially-acceptable laments and gentle hope. Mark wondered if they handed out a manual when you turned eighteen.

Occasionally he heard the rumble of discontent and distrust about the witches; because surely only magic could have taken the girls in broad daylight. And how else could someone take Imara from her bedroom?

Mostly people talked about how much they loved the missing children; and how much they would hurt if their own child vanished. They spoke of all their good memories, breathing life into them, and holding them dear.

It turned out that Hanna and Zofia were both keen footballers and had been part of the football club. They'd been at the football camp with Tyler, the second kid to go missing.

Mark felt a chill run down his spine. Three of the five kidnapped kids were linked to Damian, who was a trainer for the club. That meant they were linked to Robert…

Robert had been quiet and well-behaved since Mark had rescued him from the prison. Mark had assumed the quiet had been because of a truce… or had he still been scheming in the background? Had Will been right to accuse the demon? Mark felt sick that he chose to be so blind.

Mark spotted Damian, arriving behind his aunt and her girlfriend. He determinedly made his way to his boyfriend, but hesitated as he noticed Damian's red eyes.

Mark heart ached in response to his boyfriend's evident pain. "Are you alright?" Mark asked, wishing he could phrase it better.

"Yeah." Damian said, his eyes looking a brighter blue against the redness from crying. When he turned his gaze to Mark, he looked like he was drowning and needed someone to save him. Mark hadn't seen him look like that since he nearly died in winter…

"The police came round this morning." Miriam said. "Those girls were part of the football club, and they had the same questions, and suspicions."

"Oh Damian, I'm so sorry." Mark said, taking his boyfriend's hand and lacing their fingers together.

Damian remained silent, watching Aunt Maggie and Miriam drift away to join the adults. When they were a safe distance away, he swallowed nervously. "What if it's my fault?"

"What?"

"More awful things are happening to people, and it's like I'm the centre of it again." Damian confessed quietly.

"But... you're no longer cursed." Mark said, thinking back at all the deaths and disasters that used to stew around Damian. "That ended when Robert got his way."

"Having a demon possess me isn't exactly free from problems." Damian muttered. "What if he's doing something? I should never have joined the football club. It was irresponsible bringing him so close to so many innocent kids."

Mark was about to argue that he shouldn't stop living his life just because of Robert; but in hindsight of everything that had happened, maybe Damian was right about being more cautious.

"I was starting to think... maybe he was on our side... that he wasn't completely reprehensible..."

Damian sighed. "He's just played me for a fool again."

Mark thought things through. There was only one person who could offer answers. "Come with me." He said, pulling Damian away to the edge of the park.

Damian followed willingly. They walked until they had left the crowds behind.

"I need to speak to Robert." Mark said, anxiety prickling at his senses.

Damian frowned but nodded. He closed his eyes, and when he opened them again, his pupils were as black as night.

"Mark, long time no see." Robert said with his usual, seductive smile. He glanced down at their interlaced hands and hummed with delight. "I was wondering how long it would take you to cave."

Mark tried to pull his hand away, but Robert tightened his grip, twisting his arm and drawing him closer, until they were nearly touching.

"This isn't funny, Robert."

"I'm simply playing a part." Robert crooned in his ear. "Everyone just watched you drag your boyfriend away for a little privacy. Anything other than close contact would be suspicious."

"I don't care what people say." Mark argued, trying to break the demon's grip but it was impossible.

"Oh, I'm not so sure about that. I've heard so many rumours about how the witches aren't doing enough to help the kidnapped sprogs; or that they are behind the disappearances... I can't imagine you taking *that* sitting down."

Mark was hyper-aware of Robert, as he tilted his head into the crook of his neck. The demon took a single slow breath, but the intimacy of it all made Mark shudder. Everything about the demon invited him, and it would be so easy to give in.

Sensing a change in the tension, Robert pulled back, meeting Mark eye-to-eye. His black pupils were filled with a dark, distracting fire. He gave one of his crooked smiles, then leant in and pressed his lips against Mark's.

Disgust at what he was doing came crashing into Mark. He instinctively reached for his magic, and sent an electric shock into Robert.

The demon yelped and jumped backwards, his legs caught on the bench behind him, and he landed squarely on his arse. He glared up at Mark, accusation clear in his eyes.

"You shouldn't have done that." Mark said croakily.

"And you could have stopped me anytime you wanted." Robert countered, running his fingertips across his lips.

"It was a mistake. I won't let it happen again." Mark swore.

"Well, I don't believe that for a minute." Robert muttered. "So, what did you bring me out here for, if not to have your wicked way with me?"

"I need to know the truth." Mark said, crossing his arms. "Did you have anything to do with the missing kids?"

"Really? You think I had a part in that?" Robert pushed himself up and wiped the dirt off his trousers.

"It's not hard to believe. You told me that you like to get witches while they're young, and train them up to be loyal to you." Mark argued. "I never met the kids; they might be magical prodigies."

Robert waved a hand dismissively. "Sure, young witches, about your age. I've got no use for these infants, no matter how amazing they are."

"They're like, six and seven years old. They're not infants."

"Stupid human, they are to me. People don't become useful until they are at least fifteen."

Mark suspended his relief, running over what had been said – demons couldn't lie, but they could avoid telling the truth. He'd learnt his lesson after Silvaticus betrayed him. And Robert had been very clever at not answering him directly.

"Robert, tell me straight. Did you take these kids, or help someone else?" Mark pressed.

Robert perched on the end of the bench. "You know my name, aren't you tempted to use it? You could force me to answer you. You could force me to do practically anything, I would be your puppet."

The demon's real name sat on Mark's tongue, and he could tell it was a word of power. It was everything, and it laid the demon bare. He had to confess that it was an undeniable temptation to wield such authority over Robert.

Mark swallowed it back down. "I'm not like you, I don't force anyone to do anything."

Robert looked hurt, but snorted. "You're more manipulative than you think."

"Robert…"

"No, I had nothing to do with the kids' disappearances. You'll have to look somewhere else for your villain."

Chapter Fourteen

The vigil finished about five in the afternoon, which gave the families plenty of time to get home before curfew, for those that wanted to obey it.

As soon as they got home, Mark dragged Michelle up onto the moors. They pedalled their bikes under the hot summer sun, following the familiar tracks. He wanted to get away from the house; but more than that, he wanted to distract himself from that moment with Robert.

Mark pushed his bike harder and faster, kicking up dirt and stones, that spattered against his legs. The back of his neck burned in the summer sun, and his heart hammered under the stress. It still didn't seem enough to take the edge off.

Eventually, they reached their favourite spot by the river, and Mark reluctantly stopped.

"Alright." Michelle said, rather breathlessly. "Wanna talk about it, cuz?"

"I just wanted to get away from t'house." Mark said.

"Yeah, sure. That's it." Michelle scoffed. "Don't forget I'm the Queen of Angst. I know it when I see it."

"It's nuthin'." Mark insisted.

"Right."

Mark took a deep breath. "I want to see those kids again, see if there's anything we missed."

"Using the scrying spell?" Michelle asked.

"Um, no. I wanted to see if I could bring on a vision on demand. I don't know how they happen, but I think I'm projected there, and can interact with others." Mark replied, thinking back to the other night when the kids had reached out for him in the darkness; and when he'd interacted with Eadric...

"Well, I don't know how you do your weird vision-thing. Why didn't you ask Nanna?"

"I don't want to tire her out. She's still exhausted from confronting Konnie and her parents." Mark said, he was increasingly worried about Nanna. For the first time, he was keen to take

132

the mantle of Grand High Witch off her shoulders, regardless of what trouble it might cause him.

"Fine." Michelle shrugged. "What's the plan?"

"Nanna says magic is mostly projecting your intention, then adding power. I think it's worth a try." Mark said, thinking back to the times he had used magic without any official spells to coax them along.

"So, no plan. I like it." Michelle snorted, a little less cruelly than she used to. "Well, if you need power, but don't want to involve Nanna… are you thinking Miriam and Denise? Cos we've kinda gone the wrong way."

"Um, no. I thought just us two could do it." Mark said, nervously.

"If you're making up some random voodoo, four witches will be more balanced." Michelle whined.

"I don't think it will…." Mark bit his lip and stared at the river that rippled with light.

"You're talking more nonsense than normal. Spit it out, otherwise I'm going back to binge-watch Stranger Things." Michelle threatened.

"You're powerful, like the most powerful witch I've ever met. Not including her Grand Highness."

"Yeah, powerful witch bloodlines and all that." Michelle said.

Mark almost smiled at her Nanna-esque modesty. "Most witches have an affinity with one element. I suspect... I've suspected for a while now... that you have an affinity with two."

"Is that possible?" Michelle asked, her knowledge of natural magic even lower than Mark.

"I hadn't thought so, but my suspicions were confirmed when we last did a circle. Water and air." Mark frowned. "I wonder if Nanna noticed – she hasn't said anything."

"So, I can cover two of the four corners..." Michelle mused aloud. "Huh, go me."

"And I think I can cover the other two." Mark said quietly.

"What?"

"I always thought I had an affinity with fire, and I do; but I can't keep ignoring my connection with earth." Mark shrugged, embarrassed. "I've always noticed earth magic, been attuned to it. But maybe because it isn't as flashy as fire, I didn't think much of it. I think that's why my experiments creating that horse were always a disaster – I was only using fire magic, when the one in the demon realm was born of earth magic, too."

"So, you want just us two to create a balanced and powerful circle?" Michelle scoffed. "How do you know that's even possible?"

"We kinda did it last time, when we were scrying." Mark said, hoping he sounded more confident than he felt. "Nanna didn't put any magic into the spell; and Will was as weak as hell. It was all you and me."

"Y'know if we turn out to be exceptionally-powerful witches, Nanna is still gonna claim full credit." Michelle remarked. "Fine, let's give it a go."

Mark stood facing Michelle and closed his eyes. He reached out, drawing on fire magic out of habit. Mark berated himself, and stopped, ready to start again. He took a moment to watch Michelle, who was progressing much faster. He noted the magic that rose in blue waves. Her power was truly deafening, he could sense the strength of the deep and unstoppable oceans; and the wild energy of storms.

Mark's stance wavered, and he focussed on his own magic. He opened his senses and didn't rush towards the promise of fire. He opened himself up to the deep thrum of earth magic, it weighed heavy on his chest, the strength of iron in his limbs. Mark gently reached out for the fire, which leapt up like a familiar friend. A furnace that turned everything to ash and lava.

The combination was dizzying. Mark opened his eyes and let out a steadying breath – he'd no idea it could feel like this. The rush reminded him of when he'd used dark magic; except this time if felt natural, that he was accepting the part of himself he didn't know was missing.

It felt awkward, trying to tame the magic for a simple circle, but when it clicked, it just felt right.

Mark let Michelle keep control of the swirling power, trusting the ex-dark witch with no hesitation.

Mark slowed his breathing and tried to focus the magic, moulding it to meet his needs. He called on the missing children, and a darkness spread across the surface, but Mark could tell it was just a normal scry – still half-blocked by the kidnapper. He tried hammering through, but power alone didn't work.

Mark stood, thinking through the options, as Michelle continued to maintain the circle.

Mark focussed on the memory of his dream, reliving it in his mind; the cold, the darkness, the feel of the kids grabbing his arms. He willed it to happen again with every fibre of his being.

The sound of the cave intensified, the dripping of water down the stone walls, the breathing of the children trapped inside it. Mark was so relieved it had worked; he nearly dropped his precious hold on the spell.

"Hello?" Mark called, his voice reverberating in the enclosed space.

"You came back?" One small voice gasped.

"I did." Mark replied.

There was a shuffling in the darkness, as the five kids moved towards his voice. Mark thought they could do with a bit of light, and tried to raise a simple bit of fire, but nothing came. It felt like he had no connection to his magic in this place, and he had the same unsettled feeling he'd had in the demon realm.

"Are you taking us home?" One of the kids cried.

"Um…" Mark wondered if he could? He focussed on keeping hold of the kids and drawing them all back with him to the moors, but they slipped through his fingers, as insubstantial as ghosts, and he was standing alone in front of Michelle.

"I can get there, but my magic doesn't work. I couldn't even light a simple fire."

"Eejit." Michelle muttered, and shoved something small into his hand.

Mark looked down at the lighter and was surprised by her simple solution. "Oh."

He dove back into the spell and returned to the children who were crying because he'd left again. He used the lighter, and a little spluttering flame brought a little much needed light to things. Mark could see the five kids looking at him with wide eyes, wiping tears from their cheeks.

"You're back!"

"Are you a ghost?"

"Um, no. I'm Mark, I'm a witch." Mark explained.

"Wow, my aunties married to a witch."

"Are witches good guys?"

"I want to go home."

"We're trying our hardest to get you home, I promise. We just need your help."

"But you're a witch. You can magic us out."

"Heroes don't need help."

"Someone with magic is stopping my magic." Mark said over the chatter. "I really need any clues you can give me. Is there any way out of this cave?"

"No."

"We felt every wall."

"Maybe there's a secret door."

Mark looked around the cavern, slowed down by the kids that wanted to keep hold of him for comfort. They all chattered simultaneously, and made a bit of a racket, but they seemed healthy and unharmed, which was the most important part.

There was a pile of blankets in one corner, the material was all brown and had no symbols or logos on. No hint as to where they came from.

"That's our beds."

"It's like camping."

"I hate camping."

Mark gave them a reassuring smile, and moved onto the next corner.

"That's our bathroom."

"That's where we sh-"

"Alright." Mark interrupted. "What have you guys been doing for food?"

"Someone brings it."

"Who?"

"We don't know, we don't see them, and they don't stay."

"They always leave the food on the big square rock."

"They ring a bell when it's there."

Mark sighed, none of this was particularly useful, except it confirmed whoever was stealing the kids was keeping them safe. For now. "Do you remember anything about the person who took you?"

"No."

"They were tall."

"Everyone is tall, cos you're a midget."

"They smelt like the seaside."

"There was music."

"Yeah, music."

"Music? What did it sound like?" Mark pressed.

The kids looked at each other and some shrugged.

"Dunno."

"It made everything freeze."

"I know it! I just, can't remember."

Mark bit his lip, wondering if this was the clue he was after. The lighter was starting to get hot and was burning his thumb.

"Right, I've got to go and tell the other witches everything. I promise we'll be back." Mark let the light go out, as the kids started to whine and cry about being left alone again.

With the sound of their heart-breaking cries in his ears, he pulled away from the cold cave, and returned to the sun-baked moors.

*****

Mark wished they hadn't gone so far this afternoon, as the cycle back seemed to take forever. He was a sweaty mess by the time they got to the house, but Mark and Michelle wasted no time in tracking down Nanna, who was relaxing in the garden with a gin and tonic.

"What's got you two in a tizz?" She asked, taking in their flustered, sunburnt state.

"Um, we did a bit of magic." Mark said, glancing at Michelle conspiratorially. "I wanted to see if I could project myself into that cave again."

"Mark, that's dangerous." Nanna frowned. "That cave is protected by an unknown, powerful spell. Trying to force your way through could've killed you."

"Ah, didn't think of that." Mark said, an embarrassed blush creeping up his neck. He'd been lucky there were no repercussions for trying to force his way through the cave's defences at first.

Nanna pursed her lips. "Fine, you're alive. What happened?"

"We managed it. I got in. I managed to see a lot more this time." Mark said. "The kids are all alive and well. And the reason that no one has found them yet is because they're in a totally sealed off cavern. I think the only way in and out is by magic."

"So they might even be on a section of coast that's already been searched." Michelle said, getting to an important point. "Is there anything the covens can do to look beyond solid rock?"

Nanna chewed her lip for a moment. "Possibly. I'll let them know it's pointless searching accessible caves, and to focus further in." She pulled out her phone and tapped a quick message onto the group chat. "Was there anything else?"

"I talked to the kids." Mark replied, and gave a full account of everything they had to say.

"So, you gave your real name, and the fact that you're a witch?" Nanna said, shocked. "What happens when the kids talk about you and their kidnapper overhears? Are you asking for trouble? What if they fear you're getting too close and come for you next?"

"Good, let them come. I'd prefer a straight fight." Mark said defensively. If he drew out this shady person, it would be worth being the bait.

Nanna looked like she was gonna clip him around the ear, but Michelle beat her to it.

Mark yelped in surprise more than pain; now he had two of them picking on him.

"You're an eejit." Michelle stated.

"You're repeating yourself." Mark huffed.

"Enough." Nanna broke in before they could squabble any further.

"So, what about the kids all hearing music?" Mark asked, getting back on track. "It's like something out of The Pied Piper... he isn't real, is he?"

"There's usually some truth behind myths. If someone is using music, it might be a siren..." Nanna said thoughtfully. "I'll get Denise to put Danny on research duties, whilst he's not busy."

"Is there anything we can do?" Mark asked.

"No, you both look knackered. Get some sleep. Haven't you got that Young Farmers thing tomorrow?"

"Yeah, Mum and Dad aren't totally happy, but they're letting me go."

"Well, I know Young Farmers is usually the time to let loose; but you two best stay on guard after this debacle." Nanna warned.

Mark rolled his eyes, was it really too much to hope that Nanna would just say 'thanks for the intel' or 'good job'.

Chapter Fifteen

The Yorkshire Young Farmers' Ball was the biggest event of the season. Mark and his friends had grown up in Young Farmers, hearing all the outrageous stories, the amazing performers, the epic nights. This was the first year they were old enough to go, and Mark had been looking forward to it.

In light of what was happening in Tealford, it now seemed jarring to have a night of frivolity; but the event was organised by a council that covered the whole of Yorkshire, and they'd decided the event should go ahead as planned.

Mark's Dad drove them to the venue just outside of Northallerton. Mark and Michelle were joined by Damian and Konnie, whom Damian didn't want to leave behind, as the girl was in Yorkshire to spend time with him.

After the drama of the last time Mark had seen Konnie, the car was awkwardly silent.

"No date, Michelle?" Mark's Dad asked. "What happened to that guy from prom? I can still swing by if he needs picking up."

"Thanks, Uncle Mike, but not necessary. I didn't invite Peter – I didn't want to fill his head with any more of that romantic nonsense." Michelle pouted. "It'll cramp my style to have that puppy dog follow me around all evening."

"Hmm, 'Uncle Mike'." Dad said with a smile. "I like the sound of that."

"I thought you hated your name shortening to 'Mike'?" Mark asked.

"Ah, well, that's people in general, not my favourite niece."

"You're only niece."

"Doesn't matter, still has a nice ring to it."

Mark chuckled; both of his parents had been more than accepting of Michelle. Despite her bad attitude and dark history – or perhaps because of it – they'd made an effort to spoil her and show she was now loved and accepted.

When they arrived at the Country House that was this year's venue, they all climbed out of the car, but Dad asked Mark to stay behind.

"I want you to call me if there's even a hint of trouble." His Dad stressed. "I'm going for dinner with the other chauffeurs somewhere local. So, I mean it, if you see anything suspicious, or even have one of your funny feelings; tell me."

"Thanks, Dad." Mark said, not sure how useful his non-magical Dad would be as back-up, if anything went wrong; but appreciating the offer all the same.

"Right, well, gerroff with you." Dad said, starting his engine back up.

Mark walked up to the others, straightening his jacket and trousers. He'd learnt his lesson with his disastrous last-minute-tux and hired a suit with time to spare. It fitted perfectly and made him feel a little less of a fraud, around the many well-dressed people at this epic event.

Damian was, as always, the most stylish of the group. He had a sickeningly easy way with fashion and had a comfortable confidence that Mark could never hope to match.

Michelle had another new dress; this time a dark purple, that had a daring low back. Mark knew

147

that his Mum had relished taking her dress-shopping and came back beaming about Michelle's choices.

Konnie looked the odd-one-out. She was wearing simple white linen trousers, and a white and blue top. She looked nice, but very casual compared to everyone else. She eyed the well-dressed crowd enviously and muttered again about the short-notice she'd had for this event.

Mark was fairly sure that anything he said would only upset her further, so he left her to be comforted by Damian.

"Shall we?" He said, nodding to the main doors. "Remember, anything that happens at Young Farmers, stays at Young Farmers…"

Mark knew that there would be a formal dinner; then there would be some musicians and a DJ to finish. Harry was one of the artists performing tonight – it was one of his biggest gigs to date, and he'd promised to find Mark when he arrived later.

Mark sat down with Damian on one side, and Michelle on the other. He didn't recognise anyone else at their table, but it didn't matter, as they were all a friendly bunch, ready to have some fun. The organisers had purposefully put all the 16-year-old newcomers on the same tables, so they all shared the same, wide-eyed excitement.

Michelle seemed happy intimidating the young lad she was sat next to. Mark snorted when he overheard some of her snarky remarks, and he was glad the meanness of the old school bully seemed a thing of the past.

On the other side of Damian, Konnie looked increasingly uncomfortable, constantly playing with the locket around her neck. She didn't speak two words to any of the others at the table, and whilst they waited for their meal, she started to shrink more into Damian's side.

After dinner, everyone started to move away, heading to the hall that would include the first of the night's entertainments. Mark got a text from Harry saying he'd arrived, and he went to meet him at the main doors.

Someone grabbed his arm, and spun him firmly back. Mark was shocked to see Konnie was the one stopping him. Konnie, who'd refused to speak to him tonight.

She was shorter than Mark, but she glared up at him, not intimidated by his height. "You need to watch your back." She growled.

Mark was taken aback by the fierceness of the girl that had sat so meekly all evening. Konnie still cradled the locket she was wearing. Mark tried to get a read, to see if she was casting; but once again his focus slipped off. He guessed the locket was charmed against such things.

"Is that a threat?" He asked, trying to remain calm.

Konnie snorted. "An observation." She spat, before walking back towards the hall.

Mark stood dazed for a moment, then remembered he was supposed to be meeting Harry. What a bizarre thing to happen... why did she try and threaten him now? Did she think that because she'd managed to catch him alone, that Mark was an easy target?

After so many threats from demons and powerful dark witches, it was quite hard to take her seriously, even if she did have a few spells hidden up her sleeves.

"Hey, there you are!"

Mark heard Harry's voice and looked up to see his best friend walking in his direction. With a familiar someone in tow.

"Coira? I didn't know you were coming tonight. Are you performing too?" Mark said, trying to provide a socially-acceptable smile.

"No, I'm not. Harry invited me." Coira replied with a knowing gleam in their eye. "It's been a while since I've gone to a party."

"Right." Mark looked to his best friend for more information, but Harry seemed oblivious to any problems.

Coira seemed to read the room and made their excuse to leave. "I need the bathroom; I'll see you inside."

"You brought someone other than your girlfriend to your first ball. What were you thinking?" Mark asked.

"It's not like that, Coira's just a friend." Harry said, not impressed with Mark's accusation. "Look, it's my first gig without Sarah. Forgive me that I wanted a bit of extra support."

"I'm here to support you."

"Yeah, when you aren't doing the couple thing with Damian. Or the witch thing with Michelle." Harry grumbled. "I wanted someone here just for me, and Coira gets me. They understand the biz."

Harry's face fell, and a dark pained look crossed his face.

"What's wrong? You're normally pumped before gigs."

"Dunno, I'm just not as excited as I used to get." Harry confessed with a shrug. "Have you ever... wanted something so bad, but when you got it... I don't know how to explain it. I used to love performing, but it's starting to feel like a job, and it's like I no longer have my hobby to cheer me up. It's part of the reason me and Sarah are breaking up. I felt like she was pushing me too much."

"Oh, Harry. I had no idea." Mark said, his best friend's dark mood over the last few weeks starting to make sense.

"It's nuthin'." Harry replied. "I've had my dreams come true, and I feel guilty for not being happy."

"Maybe you need a new dream." Mark suggested. "Or a few months off professional gigs, see if you can start to enjoy it again."

"Thanks, mate."

"And I'm sorry if I made you feel guilty about Coira. It sounds like they're just the friend you need right now."

Harry's eyes welled up a bit, and he elbowed Mark hard in the ribs. "Ta."

Mark and his friends were in the main hall, the first band of the night was playing, and people were up dancing. Despite his lack of coordination and grace, even Mark joined in, as they all jumped and bounced to the energetic beat.

Damian smiled, as he witnessed Mark's dancing skills for the first time. Mark's embarrassment was cut short, when Damian caught his hand, and pulled him in for a fleeting kiss. Well, that was better than any reaction Mark had imagined.

When it was Harry's turn to perform, Mark and his friends cheered loudly, getting funny looks from those who hadn't yet heard of Not-Dave.

Harry grinned in their direction and started his first song. It was a slower pace than the last band; but as he sang, everyone stopped what they were doing, transfixed by the young lad on stage.

Harry looked confident and revelling in the moment; his music sounded as good as it always did. If Harry hadn't told him his worries earlier, Mark would never have guessed that he was unhappy.

Mark noticed Coira moving towards them, wearing a very sharp black suit, they looked comfortable at this formal event.

"Hey." Mark greeted. "I wanted to say thanks for coming to help Harry tonight."

"It was nothing." They replied. "Harry is... special."

"I don't recognise the song. Is it a new one?"

"Yes. Our collaboration proved very fruitful." Coira said, with a confident smile. They turned and fixed their bright green eyes on Harry.

After Harry's set finished, his enraptured audience had to shake off the enchanting music, and they moved away in a dazed fashion.

Mark finished cheering for his best friend, then hurried to get a drink before the next act started. He felt someone pinch his elbow, he turned sharply, but was relieved to see it was only Michelle.

"D'you want a drink?" He asked.

"If you're offering." Michelle said.

"Looks like you've got some more admirers." Mark said, nodding towards the young lads that were looking their way.

"I can't blame them. What is it Nanna says – I'm naturally beautiful – and I've got the unfair advantage of wearing make-up. They've got no hope." Michelle mused, narrowing her eyes at the group.

"None of them take your fancy?"

"Nah, they're a bunch of puppydogs. Just like Peter and Joe, that dark witch. I seem to attract 'em."

154

Michelle sighed. "Just because I've got a strong personality, doesn't mean I want to be with some weaklin' that needs coddlin'."

Mark snorted at his cousin's description. "Sometimes the 'nice guys' are stronger than you think. Just look at Damian, he's perfect."

Now it was Michelle's turn to snort. "Not my type."

There was an awkward silence, as both of them knew that Michelle's type was Robert. Mark didn't want to admit that, maybe he wasn't completely immune to Robert's charm, either...

"What were you and Konnie talking about earlier?" Michelle asked, changing the topic. "She looked pretty pissed?"

"I wouldn't say we were 'talking'." Mark glanced about, making sure the girl wasn't nearby. "She threatened me, then stormed off."

"What?"

"Yeah, told me I needed to watch my back." Mark finally got his turn at the bar and ordered a couple of cokes for them. "To be honest, threats have lost all effectiveness after putting up with you all these months."

"I'm glad to hear it." Michelle accepted her drink. "There's only one role for angsty dark witch, and I've got that covered."

Mark felt the excitement of today burn through him, and his limbs suddenly felt heavy. He found the nearest empty chair and sat down; Michelle sitting next to him.

"I can't imagine what she thinks she can pull against us. Her mother is a weak witch, and I don't think I've ever seen Konnie use magic. Still, we'll have to stay alert." Mark mused aloud, followed by a yawn.

He looked over at Michelle, who'd fallen fast asleep in her seat.

Mark felt a wave of fatigue wash over him.

"Oh sh-"

Chapter Sixteen

As Mark came to, he could see an empty room, which was so quiet after the madness of the ball. Everything else was slow to process. He remembered being surrounded by people, watching Harry's set. He'd gotten a drink with Michelle, hadn't he?

There had been disappearances, and now it was his turn to be kidnapped. This didn't look like a dank cave by the sea...

"You awake?"

Mark heard the familiar voice, but the name stayed stubbornly out of reach.

"Oi, Mark!"

Ah, so Michelle was here too. "Yeah." He replied groggily.

"This is all your fault." Michelle snapped. "I blame you."

Mark tried to take a deep breath but found it hard. He leant forward, and felt a rope tighten around his chest. As feeling returned to the rest of his body, he realised that his arms were pulled uncomfortably behind his back.

"Wha' happened?"

"Best I can figure, someone spiked our drinks." Michelle said. "I guess I'm lucky. My dabbling in drugs has made it less effective on me. Otherwise, I'd still be a drooling idiot like you."

"Mm." Mark tried to call on fire magic, to burn through the ropes; but nothing happened.

In his drugged state, he was slow to process the fact that his magic was blocked.

"It's no use, I've already tried that." Michelle snapped.

A door behind them opened and closed with a thud that was loud enough to make Mark jump.

"You're awake. Finally."

The speaker moved in front of them. They looked vaguely familiar, but Mark couldn't place them. That wasn't the case for Michelle.

"You! You little weasel."

The guy looked quite pleased with himself.

"You have no idea who you're dealing with." Michelle threatened.

"Actually, I *finally* know who I'm dealing with." He pointed at the two of them. "You really played me for a fool."

"Didn't take much playing." Michelle muttered.

"I'm sorry, who are you?" Mark asked, wanting to get some answers for his drug-addled brain.

"Who am I? Seriously!" The guy practically howled with anger, and Mark could see the dark magic ripple across his skin.

Mark tuned his head to Michelle, as best he could. "Joe, the dark witch guy?" He guessed.

"That's him." Michelle confirmed.

"Oh." Mark said, then paused as his thoughts caught up. "Where are the others?"

"What others?"

"The kids, where are they?" Mark demanded, struggling against his bonds.

"Ha, you spoutin' nonsense, bro. Is that the drugs, or it that normal for you?" Joe came uncomfortably close to Mark, no fear that he might retaliate.

Mark strained to turn his head enough to look at Michelle. "No kids?"

"Looks like." She replied.

"So, why are we tied to chairs?" Mark asked, struggling to understand what was happening.

"Because *She* wants you." Joe said enthusiastically. "And *we* have delivered you; we will be rewarded."

"Crap, I'm guessing he means-"

"Edith." Mark finished. "That's just great…"

Mark reached for his magic again, but it was still missing; a great hole in his being that left him unbalanced.

"Come on, Joe, she'll kill us if you hand us over." Mark tried to reason. "It's not too late, you can still let us go."

"No, no, no. She doesn't want to kill Michelle, she just wants her daughter back, to be treated like the royalty she is." Joe replied, his gaze unfocussed and his movement erratic. "The boy dies, the grandson of the High Grand… Grand Witch…"

"You don't know that. She won't keep her promise, she will hurt Michelle." Mark argued.

"There's no point reasoning with him." Michelle said quietly.

Mark frowned in the direction of his cousin, who wasn't trying very hard to get them out of this situation.

"What do you get out of this deal?" Mark asked.

"Dark magic." Joe said, the words pouring out. "More dark magic. Enough for our whole coven for a year. We will be the most powerful coven in the North of England; we will be Edith's allies and her equals. She has already given us a taste."

"Edith doesn't want equals." Michelle stated coldly.

"Lies." Joe barked, surging towards Michelle, he raised his hand and slapped her so hard her head snapped back. "No, no, no. Michelle is not to be harmed."

Joe held his own reddened hand and left; the door thudding shut behind him.

"Michelle, are you alright?" Mark asked.

"I've just been slapped by some greasy little guy on a power trip." Michelle stretched her jaw to ease her painful cheek. "I suppose it's not the worst thing that's happened to me."

"Can't you… reason with him? He seemed to like you last time." Mark asked quietly, not sure who else was within earshot.

"Reason with him?" Michelle snorted. "No chance. You saw what he's like, he's high on dark magic; and possibly other drugs. His brain is fried. And you know what a dark magic hangover is like – there's no guarantee he'll be any better once sober."

"Do you really think he'll hand us over to Edith to be killed?" Mark asked, sickened that the surprisingly-normal guy he'd hung out with only couple of months ago could do such a thing.

"I think Joe and his coven wouldn't bat an eye at killing us, if it meant they could get more dark magic to fuel their habit." Michelle sighed. "I know a little of what that's like; and these guys are much further gone than I was."

They both fell silent when the door opened again, and a young woman entered, carrying a jug carefully.

She looked vaguely familiar, and she turned to face Mark, he drew a sharp breath. She was the barmaid who'd served him at the ball and was still wearing her work uniform.

"You need another dose. Joe says you're getting feisty." She said, her words and movements were steady, but there was something unfocussed about her eyes.

"You don't have to do this." Mark pleaded. "If you help us get out of here, we can protect you from Edith."

The woman laughed at his offer. "Edith makes us strong, why would we betray her?"

She grabbed Mark's hair and yanked his head back, pouring the liquid in his mouth. He felt like he was going to choke, and he coughed and tried to spit it out; but he was already feeling the numbing effect of the potion.

Mark was vaguely aware of Michelle swearing violently at the woman, before everything faded to black again.

*****

The next time Mark came to, he was still in the same room, with only Michelle for company. Music was being played at volume somewhere nearby, the bass sending vibrations through the chair he was stuck to.

Mark was grateful they hadn't been packed off to Edith yet; but his gratitude was a brief, flickering light. He still couldn't connect to his magic. It was almost painful to be apart from it.

"You awake yet?" Came Michelle's voice.

"Yeah." Mark replied wearily.

"Your powers of persuasion are pretty shitty. How on earth did you get me to join your side?"

"Mm, I wasn't at my best tonight." Mark agreed. "Maybe it was because you were still a good person. It might be a lost cause with these guys."

"Hmph."

"How's your cheek?" Mark asked.

"It still hurts. I'm gonna have an awesome bruise to show for it." Michelle muttered, bitter that her old friend had stooped so low.

"So, the kids aren't here." Mark said with a disappointed sigh. "It would have been worth all this if they were. We could be rescuing them right now. This means there's like, another villain hiding in the shadows."

"We'll find them." Michelle promised. "We just need to get out of here, first. Got any of those bright ideas of yours, that always go sideways?"

"Sorry to disappoint. I'm still working on it." Mark bit his lip. "Best I have so far, is to wait for the potion's effect to fade. All we need is a smidge of magic; then we can create a circle…"

"Then we can fight our way out of a coven of second-rate dark witches." Michelle shook her head. "I don't know how you come up with these brilliant plans!"

"If you've got a better idea, I'd love to hear it." Mark sighed. "If that's the same potion as before, you'll have access to your magic before I do. Be ready."

"Yes, sir." Michelle said, her voice dripping with sarcasm.

What felt like an age later, the door opened, and Joe and the woman re-entered the room. They untied the ropes that bound Mark and Michelle to the chairs but kept their hands behind them. With some awkward manoeuvring, they were pulled to their feet and pushed through the door.

After hours of being stuck in one position, Mark's legs spasmed, and he staggered. Joe was smaller and weaker than him, but he used his borrowed dark magic to half-carry Mark down a dim corridor. Mark could practically see the oily residue on Joe's arms, both revolting and pure temptation.

"Where are we going?" Mark demanded.

"Our ride is here. We're taking you to Edith." Joe crowed.

The music got louder, as Mark was pushed into a large room, where the rest of Joe's coven hovered. They all looked at their prisoners, and Mark felt a wave of excitement ripple through the room. There were about a dozen witches, all stood, ready. Dark magic curled about them, infesting their auras.

Mark noticed the hatred that burnt in their eyes for him and Michelle – the natural witches that dared to be more powerful than them, because they had the good fate to be related to the Grand High Witch.

The dark witches' emotions were so close to the surface, broiling along with the dark magic. It would only take a single match to set them all ablaze.

Mark reached out with his senses, but still couldn't connect to his own power. He also couldn't feel any hint of Michelle's. Which left them helpless.

Without magic, Mark reminded himself. Not entirely helpless. He still had his fists, and Michelle still had her... well, her ability to scare the life out of her enemies.

Mark managed to look in Michelle's direction and met her eye. He could tell that she was thinking the same thing. They'd fight their way out, if they had to.

Michelle threw herself at the female witch, both of them making a sickening thud against the wall.

With his hands still tied behind his back, Mark kneed Joe in the gut, making the man crumple.

There was a hiss from the remaining coven, and a moment's pause as they started to raise their offensive spells.

Mark only had moments before he lost his advantage, and he rugby-tackled the nearest witch, stunning at least one more. And then the wave of dark magic came.

Mark knew they'd been gifted magic from Edith, but he hadn't expected it to be so powerful. It made the very air thick and hard to breath. It was beyond witches. It was more like… a demon.

Half of the building exploded in a blinding light. Mark cowered as large chunks of masonry and twisted metal girders fell through the dust-filled air. There were screams, when they landed on the dark witches that surrounded them. But Mark's attention was locked on the gaping hole.

A creature of fire and fury roared and brought down its claws without mercy. It was truly massive, as tall as the building. It's reptile-shaped head snaked through the gloom, and everywhere it moved, fires sprung up, eating at the destruction.

The dark witches that survived the initial blast tried to rally, but their borrowed magic dissipated into the air, useless against this force of nature.

Mark's heart thudded as the dark witches' spells crashed against the demon's side, proving insignificant.

"HE IS OURS." The demon roared, fire bursting from its maw.

Mark coughed as the smoke thickened. The fire had well-and-truly caught and was eating up the old warehouses. He felt a stab of panic – in his current state he had no magical protection from fire, and it felt like an ironic way to go.

Luckily, Michelle had kept her head. She'd also managed to get a knife and cut their restraints. She then dragged her cousin towards the exit.

The fresh air had never felt so good, and Mark fell to his knees, breathing it in and trying to cough up the cloying smoke from his lungs.

When he raised his head, he saw a single figure making their way towards them. No longer huge, they were very average-sized, but far from average-looking.

"Thank you." Mark managed, before everything went black.

Chapter Seventeen

When Mark woke up, he found himself on the sofa of his living room. He jerked to sit up, still plagued by a sense of danger; but the most dangerous thing was his Mum with her knitting needles.

"Oh, you're awake, love." Mum sounded relieved. She put down her knitting. "How are you feeling?"

"Sore." Mark replied honestly, his voice hoarse from smoke inhalation. His chest hurt from the ropes that had bound him, and he could see bruising at his wrists. "What happened?"

"You were attacked by dark witches. Michelle and Damian brought you home." Mum said. "You were a bit heavy to get upstairs, so we let you sleep on the sofa. Now, what hurts?"

His Mum switched into nurse-mode and checked Mark over for injuries. "Right, nothing serious. Just bad bruising, perhaps torn muscle in your shoulder. If that keeps bothering you, we'll take you to the doctor. For now, I want you to rest today, and drink Nanna's miracle tea."

"How's Michelle?" Mark asked.

"She's fine. Just bruises. I tried to get Damian to stay the night, but he insisted on going home." Mum said, picking up her knitting again. "Nanna said she wanted to see you this morning."

"Yeah." Mark mumbled, he imagined she would.

After he'd showered the best he could with his stiff arms, Mark headed over to Nanna's side of the house, where she and Michelle were sitting in the living room. As soon as he arrived, they switched off the tv.

"So… Michelle filled me in on everything. How the dark witches spiked you, and were planning on taking you to Edith. And how you were rescued by Robert." Nanna said succinctly.

"Yeah, and how you fainted like some damsel-in-distress." Michelle snorted. "Robert got a kick out of carrying you home."

Mark swore beneath his breath, not liking that he'd been so vulnerable in front of the demon.

"It was smoke inhalation. What happened to the witches? Did they survive?" Mark asked quietly, not wanting the answer.

"Dunno, we didn't stick around to find out." Michelle replied vaguely.

Mark's stomach still dropped. He knew they weren't good people; but no one deserved to die. To think Robert may have killed them for him, made him feel sick to his very bones.

"Well, I suppose it's confirmed our fears about Konnie and her family." Mark said as soon as he could speak, forcefully changing the subject.

Nanna and Michelle exchanged looks.

"Not quite." Michelle muttered.

"Robert told us that Konnie saw you both get taken, and she immediately tracked down Damian, so they could help." Nanna said. "It turned out that she suspected her parents would act last night, whilst you were both far away from me and the protection of our coven."

"What?"

"Yeah." Michelle shrugged. "She's not the bad guy after all."

"So... when she told me to watch my back... she was trying to warn me?" Mark frowned.

The girl had come across as threatening and aggressive, and had done nothing to gain his trust last night. Until she sent the cavalry to save them.

"Yeah, Konnie said she knew her mum had been making some more of that delightful potion, and had overheard her making plans with another witch." Michelle tilted her head. "I suppose we're lucky the angsty little thing was there last night."

"We're gonna have to press pause on this mystery. We're heading to Denise's to find out what Danny has found out." Nanna said, standing up. "I know you guys are supposed to be resting, but it's only a short drive."

Mark and Michelle both grimaced at the prospect of Nanna's awful driving.

*****

They arrived at Denise's without too many new bruises.

Denise ushered them into the kitchen, where Danny sat waiting for them. He was starting to look more like his old self, having shaved, and wearing clean and unrumpled clothes. Danny still had a haunted look about him, but when he noticed them enter, his patronising air was back.

"Danny, it's good to see you out of your prison cell." Nanna said, as they all sat around the table.

"Thanks Nanna. When mother said you needed my specialised assistance…"

Mark glanced at Michelle and rolled his eyes. Yeah, he'd not missed this at all.

"So, what have you found?" Nanna asked, after allowing Danny to finish.

"Well, I've been investigating demons and creatures that are associated with singing to bewitch their prey, just in case young Mark's tip is accurate." Danny gave a knowing smile. "There were quite a few, but I've managed to rule several out. Sirens and selkies don't seem to fit the profile. Whereas kelpies…"

"Kelpies?" Mark froze to the spot.

Danny didn't look pleased at the interruption. "As I was saying, a kelpie is a logical suspect. Especially since *someone* released one from prison recently."

Mark sat, reeling over the facts. If it was a kelpie stealing these children; it was all his fault. He'd been so preoccupied with Robert that he'd let them go – more than that, he'd physically broken the kelpie out of a demon prison – and completely forgotten about it.

He remembered the innocent-looking creature, looking similar to a black horse, with a seaweed mane.

"I've not come across a kelpie before..." Nanna said quietly.

"Yes, mother said she suspected as much. I took the liberty to research who might be able to help us, or offer vital information." Danny paused, making sure the group was hanging on his every word. "I've been in touch with the MacGregor family, they have a long-standing history with kelpies. When I told them about our problem, they insisted on coming down immediately. They'll be here first thing tomorrow."

Mark sighed. He really hated it when Danny proved how very useful and competent, he was. Especially now it seemed like he was cleaning up Mark's mess.

"I don't know if you heard, with what happened..." Denise paused. "Three more children went missing."

"Three?" Mark gasped, the kelpie was making a mockery of them.

"We think that, whatever creature is behind the disappearances, knows that we are onto them, thanks to Mark's visit to the cave." Danny explained. "They know there's only a short time to do what they have to do."

*****

The following morning, Mark, Michelle and Nanna all returned to Denise's house. Mark could tell Nanna was agitated, facing a creature she hadn't met before in her long career as the Grand High Witch. Turning to people she didn't know, for help.

Mark had noticed that Nanna's go-to for potentially uncomfortable situations, was to go big. She always demonstrated her power early, to stamp out any questions or objections. And she wore her magic now like a cloak, a storm barely-contained. Mark only hoped she didn't exhaust herself again.

It turned out that going in with all magical guns blazing was pointless. The MacGregor family weren't witches, and they couldn't read the power radiating off Nanna.

Nanna pouted, and let her magic drop away.

The MacGregor family looked very normal – Mark had been expecting something along the line of Indiana Jones – intellectuals wearing leather hats and jackets – but these people were simply dressed in jeans and tops, not a whip in sight.

"I'm Ron," The eldest guy said, with a Falkirk accent. "These are my kids. My son, Oliver; and daughter, Phemy. Thanks for getting in touch with us."

"Thanks for coming at such short notice." Nanna replied.

"Well, Danny made quite the case, it sounded urgent. How many kids have gone missing?" Ron asked.

"Eight."

"Then we need to act quickly, kelpies will gather nine children, before eating them."

"Why nine?" Mark asked.

"Why do creatures do anything? Because it's in its nature." Oliver MacGregor spoke up. "There are stories about a kelpie with nine children on its back, and the tenth child that escaped. But it's just a story – people probably trying to make sense of what they don't understand."

"That's not really relevant information, right now." Ron interrupted his son.

"What do we need to know? How do we stop them before another kid goes missing?" Nanna asked.

"Kelpies are a type of water demon, and they can turn into a horse, or take human form. They're normally creatures of habit, but this one seems to be unusual. I've never known one to target a town so far away from water." Ron frowned.

Mark grimaced. He had a horrible suspicion he knew why this particular kelpie had come to Tealford. There was no escaping it, this was all his fault. Robert had even tried to warn him that the kelpie wasn't good, and Mark had just ignored his advice.

"So, they're probably residing close to water." Oliver added.

"We think they're hiding in caves by the coast." Nanna said. "We've narrowed it down to a beach with stones, rather than sand. I've got witches up and down the county on this."

"And it's likely they're maintaining a human persona in town, it's the only reason I can think of them staying so far away from their natural habitat." Ron said. "Do you know of anyone who's recently arrived?"

"Well, there's Konnie, and her parents." Michelle offered, immediately. "They're suspicious as hell."

"And there's Coira." Mark said, suddenly feeling uneasy. "They're keen on music, too."

Coira had their quirks, the same as any teenager, but despite the fractures they'd caused between Harry and Sarah, they seemed like a nice person. It was hard to imagine they could be a children-eating shape-shifter. But... Mark had thought the kelpie was an innocent victim, when he'd released it from prison.

"Do you have any photos of the suspects? Your witches can use them, see if anyone along the coast has noticed them coming and going a lot." Ron suggested.

"Um, yeah. We have photos of Konnie and Coira from the bowling night." Mark said, pulling out his phone. "We don't have any of Mr and Mrs Lykaois."

He pulled up his photos and added them to the coven leader's Whatsapp group, tapping out a quick explanation.

Michelle was scrolling through her phone. "I found a news article about Konnie's miraculous recovery. It's got a photo of her parents – not great, but should do the job. I'll send it you."

Mark nodded, impressed by his cousin's resourcefulness. He added the third photo.

"So, once we find the kelpie, how do we stop them?" Nanna asked, moving things along.

"My daughter Phemy is the expert on this part, but you'll have to excuse us – she's mute after a fae curse. I'm sure she'll let us know if I say anything wrong." Ron said, looking embarrassed. "You need to 'tame' them, by putting a bridle on them. All kelpies have their own bridle – most are hidden, because it's their weak point. Regular, leather bridles can sometimes work; but ones forged from iron are best, if you have a skilled blacksmith?"

Everyone looked pointedly at Nanna.

She swore under her breath. "Fine, I'll contact Derek."

The MacGregor family looked bemused at the reaction, but the father eventually carried on.

"Once you have a bridle ready, you have to trap the kelpie on dry land, where it will be at its weakest. Once the bridle is on, you will have full control of the kelpie."

Phemy coughed, and frowned at her father's words.

"Fine, you'll have some control over the kelpie. Like any horse, they still have their moments of wildness, and can still place curses, which can be nasty... but it will no longer be a threat to children,

179

and you'll be able to transport it somewhere secure. If you don't have suitable facilities here, we have a secure compound back home."

Mark took a slow breath, with the help of one of the demons, he could return the kelpie to the demon prison back in the Brimcliff Duchy. Yet, even the thought of that was abhorrent. He remembered the pain and despair that seeped through every damp wall. He remembered the eyes of every creature he passed, all filled with fear and begging for it to end. At the time, he'd thought that he didn't even want his worst enemy in there. And he didn't want to put the kelpie back. Whatever the MacGregors were offering had to be better than that.

"Right. Let's get cracking." Nanna said, wrapping things up.

*****

As they drove back, Mark tried to call on his magic. It sounded like they would need to act quickly, and he was relieved that the magic-numbing potion was wearing off. His power didn't come completely easy, it seemed slow and a little reluctant, but it was there. Mark only hoped he was fully-recovered in time for their clash with the kelpie.

His thoughts were broken as Nanna swerved sharply up their drive, throwing Mark off balance. He gritted his teeth and was glad the journey was almost over.

As they drove up to the house, Mark spotted a familiar figure standing on Nanna's side of the house waiting for them. Damian.

When Mark got out of the car and got closer, his momentary excitement at seeing his boyfriend faded. Robert.

"Demon." Nanna greeted; the single word full of threats.

"Witch." Robert returned. "I want to speak with your grandson."

Nanna crossed her arms. "Uh huh, I'm sure."

"Look, haven't I proven that you can trust me, at least where your grandkids are involved?" Robert argued. "Didn't I rescue them last night?"

"The two grandkids that both got hooked on dark magic, because of you?" Nanna clarified.

Mark could see Nanna's magic rising in time with her temper. He didn't need her doing something stupid now, when they were all preparing for a bigger fight.

"Nanna, stop. I'll deal with this." Mark said. He nodded to Michelle, hoping she'd get the hint and take Nanna inside.

Michelle was busy looking at Robert with pure venom. When they went into the kitchen, the door slammed behind them. Mark could hear raised voices, and he could easily guess who they were complaining about. A part of him felt happy that Michelle had found a topic she and Nanna could agree on, and was openly communicating for the first time in weeks – verbally cursing every bone in Robert's body.

Mark moved away from the house, and hovered by the edge of the garden. He could feel Robert following him.

"What do you want?" Mark asked, tersely.

"A little gratitude." Robert looked taken aback by Mark's mood. "And if that isn't available, I'd settle for knowing you are alright."

"We're both fine." Mark replied, then corrected himself. "We'll heal."

"I can help you with that if you want." Robert offered his hand, dark magic rippling across the surface. He reached out to Mark.

"Don't touch me!" Mark snapped, jumping back.

Robert looked baffled. "What's wrong?"

"Nowt."

"This isn't playing out how I imagined it. I mean, my favourite fantasy involved you throwing yourself at me, to thank me for saving you. At the very least, I expected you to be happy to see me." Robert frowned. "Not this downright hostility."

"How can you see yourself as the hero in this scenario? You didn't have to kill those people." Mark snapped.

"Excuse me?" Robert pouted. "Those people were dark witches, intent on killing you. I read the spells they were casting. It was them, or you, and I chose you."

"I don't care what the intentions of some witches high on dark magic were. You can't go around killing people!" Mark shouted. "You could have incapacitated them, or..."

"I've been around for two thousand years, and have seen every manner of battle. It's not like you see in films. The odds of successfully extracting you without neutralising the threat were slim. I couldn't risk it." Robert said coldly. "Besides, it's in my nature to kill. I'm the evil demon, after all."

"Yes, but those deaths are on my conscience, now. I don't want anyone to die on my behalf."

Mark's voice was raising, trying to impress his human morals on this thick-headed demon was proving futile. "I don't know what possessed you-"

"Because *I'm in love with you!*" Robert shouted back.

Mark froze, staring into the demon's black eyes. He'd not been expecting that, and it made him feel extremely uneasy. "You don't know a thing about love." He snapped defensively.

"I know more about the many types of love, and know them in more depth than you could ever dream." Robert said quietly.

Mark glared at the demon, a million thoughts and feelings rushing through him, but none that made any sense. "I need you to leave." He said, croakily.

"Mark..." Robert stepped closer to him, trying to reason with him.

"I need you to leave." Mark repeated, his world spinning.

"No, I think I should stay." Robert took another step closer, until they were chest to chest. He reached out, his hand tracing the line of Mark's tense jaw, before leaning in to kiss...

Mark closed his eyes, and said the demon's name. When he opened his eyes, he noticed Robert's black pupils had gone hard. The demon shrank away from him.

"As you command." He said bitterly, his voice a thousand heart-breaks. *"Siþwegas."*

There was a flash of white light, and Robert vanished.

Chapter Eighteen

Mark went back into the house, feeling completely numb. He ignored Michelle's and Nanna's attempts to question him about Robert's visit.

A very welcome distraction came in the shape of a message from the covens' Whatsapp group. With the help of the photos he'd sent earlier, they'd been able to stir some comments from the general public.

A restaurant owner in a small village north of Scarborough had seen something they thought odd. The same person kept coming in daily, for an increasing amount of takeaway meals. He'd originally thought they were just another tourist, but instead of disappearing after a week or two, they kept coming. The mystery person was a point of discussion for his regulars – the village was small enough that everyone knew everybody, and they were fairly sure they weren't living locally.

"It's Coira." Mark announced, his gut twisting. "I have to call Harry."

Mark went out into the garden for some privacy for what was sure to be an awkward call. Mark tried to call Harry, but there was no answer. He hung up and sent him a message.

'I need to talk to you asap. Please stay away from Coira.'

Mark tapped his phone, maybe he should head over to Harry's place.

His phone buzzed with a new message from his best friend: *'You guys need to accept that they're part of my life now.'*

'This isn't about your love life. They're not who you think. I need to talk to you.'

'I know them better than you do.'

Mark swore, and tried to call Harry again, but he still didn't answer. He was worried that if they were with Harry, Coira might see whatever message he sent; but Mark had to tell him everything.

'They are a kelpie!'

Mark's heart hammered, as he waited for a reply.

'A water spirit, I know. They told me.'

That was the last thing Mark expected. How long had his best friend known? Mark was hurt that Harry hadn't said anything, especially as he'd been very open about the whole demon-possessed boyfriend thing.

'They're dangerous.'

Mark could see that Harry had read his message, but no reply came. He used some of Nanna's choicest swearwords, and headed back inside.

"I think Harry's in trouble. He said that he knew Coira was a kelpie. I don't get why he's not more worried, he's always been vocal about how much he distrusts Rob- um, demons." Mark fretted.

Michelle snorted. "It's amazing how blind guys get about people they like."

"Right, go round to his house, boy. See if you can talk some sense into him. Or at the very least, protect him from Coira until we're ready." Nanna said, already looking pale and tired. "Derek will have the bridle ready in a couple of hours. We'll meet at Denise's this evening and go from there."

Mark nodded, and went out to get his bike, with Michelle in tow. They set off at a fierce pace, down the winding country roads. Quarter an hour later they arrived at Harry's house. They threw their bikes down on the front garden, and Mark banged on the door until it was wrenched open.

"Mark, what on earth is this about?" Harry's mum asked.

"Hi, Mrs Johnson." Mark paused, gasping for breath. "Harry… is Harry in?"

"No, dear, he's not. Is everything alright?"

Mark thought briefly of telling Mrs Johnson the truth, but he didn't know if she'd believe him. "Um, yeah. I just need to see him. Do you know where he is?"

"Yes, dear, He's off with his new friend, Coira." Mrs Johnson pursed her lips, as though she had more to say.

"Are you alright, Mrs Johnson?" Mark asked.

"Well, I know it's none of my business, and Coira is lovely, but… I do miss Sarah. Do you think they'll patch things up?"

Mark wondered that, too. He missed how easy things used to be; but he didn't know how keen Sarah would be to take Harry back after he ditched her for a child-eating water demon. "I don't know, Mrs Johnson. I hope so."

"Do you know where Coira and Harry went to?" Michelle asked, getting them back on topic.

"Oh yes, Harry was quite excited. It's the first time he's been invited to see Coira's house. He warned me that it's in the middle of nowhere, so not to worry if he misses my calls."

Harry and Michelle exchanged looks.

"Thanks, Mrs Johnson. We'd best be off." Mark said, smiling politely to hide his fear. They were too late.

"What now?" Michelle asked. "You could call Robert, and get him to use the demon road to get us to the coast."

Mark blanched at the idea. "Um, he's ignoring my calls. I don't know where he is."

"What? He was practically falling over himself to help you a few hours ago. What did you do?"

"Nowt. We had a falling out." Mark said vaguely.

"Great time to piss off the demon most likely to help us." Michelle snapped.

"I thought you hated him."

"Yeah, it doesn't mean I'm above using him when necessary." Michelle shook her head. "This is for *Harry*."

"We need to go to Denise's." Mark said, pulling his bike off Harry's front lawn.

"What, you're going to wait for the bridle and the cavalry to assemble?" Michelle asked with disgust.

"I never said that."

*****

By the time they reached Denise's house, Mark thought his legs were going to fall off. They'd cycled without a break, knowing that every minute was precious.

Denise opened the door, looking surprised at their appearance. "Is everything alright?"

"No, Coira got to Harry before we could." Mark said. "Can we see Danny?"

Denise narrowed her eyes, knowing something must be amiss if Mark *wanted* to see her patronising son. "He's in the kitchen. You're not about to do something stupid?"

"Yeah, probably." Mark replied, heading towards the kitchen.

Danny was sat with Phemy MacGregor, having an in-depth discussion about something. Phemy replied to Danny's questions, signing quickly.

"Hm, that's interesting." Danny said.

"What's that, dear?" Denise asked.

"Oh, Phemy was just telling me about the first MacGregor to steal a kelpie bridle from the local Loch Slochd. The kelpie turned into a beautiful woman, and they, um, actually became friends." Danny blushed a little.

"That's not what she signed." Michelle chuckled.

"You can sign?" Mark asked.

"What, you can't?" Michelle retorted.

"Danny, can we speak to you in private, please?" Mark said.

Danny looked surprised, but led the way out into the garden. "Very well, what did you want to talk about?"

"Harry's in trouble. The kelpie has taken him. That makes it nine kidnappings – you heard what the MacGregors said. We have to go after them now."

"Isn't Harry a bit older than the other kids that were taken?" Danny frowned.

"Yeah, I don't know why they've changed their plans. Maybe they know we're onto them, and can't be choosy." Mark replied. "It doesn't matter what the reason is, we have to go now."

"Nanna's farrier friend will have the bridle ready in an hour or so. That's the only known way to stop a kelpie; it would be wisest to wait." Danny reasoned.

"We might not have an hour." Mark argued. "Besides, the bridle is the only thing that worked for the non-magical MacGregors. I think between us, we pack a bit more of a punch."

"So, what, you just want to drive over there and hope for the best?" Danny shook his head at their lack of planning.

"Not exactly." Mark said.

He looked at Danny, and could see the moment the teacher understood what Mark was saying.

"Ah. When you said you wanted to speak to me, you really needed to speak to Silvaticus. This sounds familiar." Danny crossed his arms.

"Well, he has been behaving himself for the last few weeks. And... we're desperate. This is for *Harry* and those eight other innocent children." Mark stressed. "Please can we speak with Silvaticus?"

"Fine." Danny muttered. He didn't immediately shift into the demon he'd been living in fear of for the last couple of months. For the first time, Mark thought he looked scared, he was apprehensive of allowing the demon to take control.

It was obvious when Silvaticus took over. The nervous energy stilled, and he became a calm pool of power.

"Mark. Michelle." He greeted them.

"Silvaticus." Mark tried to appear equally calm in front of the demon that had betrayed him. "Did you hear everything?"

"I did, indeed. I assume you want my help with the kelpie you released from prison."

"Not quite, Michelle and I will deal with the kelpie. We would like your help to get there, and to get the children to safety." Mark said.

Silvaticus gazed at them with his unsettling, and unblinking black eyes. "Very well. Where are we going?"

"Hayburn Wyke, just North of Scarborough."

The demon went to move, but stopped, and turned back to Mark. "I am about to open the demon road. Do I have your permission to take you through it?"

Mark heard Michelle snort with amusement behind him. He realised that Silvaticus was making an extra effort to be polite after the last time, when he'd dragged Mark into the demon realm with no warning.

"Thank you. You have our permission." Mark said, matching his manners.

"*Sipwegas.*"

There was a flash of white light, and then the familiar dark red nothingness of the demon road. Moments later, there was another flash.

A fresh sea breeze tugged at their clothes. They were surrounded by green trees that ended abruptly, with only a hint of grey stone to show where the ground fell away into a steep cliff.

Water was everywhere – there was the steady crash of waves below; and the constant rumble of waterfalls nearby. No wonder Coira was drawn to this place.

"What now?" Michelle asked.

"Our priority is getting the kids out safely." Mark stated. As much as he wanted to go in guns blazing and rescue Harry, those kids were innocent and didn't deserve any of this. "From what they said, they are normally alone in the cavern. If we are lucky, Coira won't be there."

"If? Luck? Maybe?" Michelle tilted her head. "Yeah, definitely one of your half-baked ideas."

Mark ignored his cousin's taunts. "The cavern is completely sealed physically, and bars against our magic. Can you break through the spell, Silvaticus? Or transport directly within?"

Silvaticus looked at the ground for a long few moments before replying. "It is likely I can break the spell; but I won't be able to blindly transport into the cave."

Mark's hopes fell a little, until he noticed Silvaticus rolling up his sleeves.

He'd forgotten the demon's affinity for earth, and staggered as the ground began to rumble. After all the things Mark had seen, he was still in awe of Silvaticus' power, as huge chunks of earth and rock tore themselves free and started to form a new mountain.

Mark's revery was broken by Michelle elbowing him in the ribs.

"Isn't this supposed to be your forte?"

Mark blinked, feeling foolish. It still felt weird to embrace his connection to earth magic, and he felt like a fraud next to someone of Silvaticus' calibre, but he dutifully got to work.

Mark could see that Silvaticus was forming a ramp, leading down to the location of the cavern. Mark cracked his knuckles, and followed the demon's lead.

They made quick work of the topsoil, but the bedrock underneath was a little more stubborn.

Between the two of them, they managed to create a serviceable ramp. At the very bottom, was a small hole in the cavern wall. Mark could see the pale faces of the children, only imprisoned by a thin layer of dark magic.

Silvaticus closed his eyes and focussed on the spell.

Mark kept on alert, waiting for the moment Coira returned and discovered their big breakout. He knew that Michelle was at the top of the cliff, equally observant.

"It is done." Silvaticus said, calmly, opening his dark eyes.

"Come on, kids." Mark leant through the hole, he could sense the remnants of the destroyed dark magic spell. It had a vague burnt smell.

"Mark, you came back!" The kids shouted with excitement, and took no further encouragement to pour out of the gap.

"I promised we would be." Mark smiled, counting the kids as they exited. There were eight. "Where's Harry?"

Mark climbed into the cavern, and ran to each corner of the space. There was no sign of his best friend.

"Mark, it is unwise to tarry." Silvaticus reminded him.

"Harry's not here." Mark said.

"You said the priority was the children. We need to get them to safety." Silvaticus stated.

Mark climbed back out of the gap. The kids were all looking at him with varying expressions of excitement, confusion, and fear.

"Hey, did you guys see my friend? He's about as tall as me, has brown hair, tells stupid jokes?" Mark asked.

The kids shook their heads.

"No."

"No big people."

"All people are big to you, shrimp."

The kids chattering replies were cut short from a scream above.

"Incoming!"

Mark scrambled to the top of the ramp, and found Michelle backing away from the cliff's edge.

He could spy a dark shadow moving at speed across the surface of the sea. It danced with grace along the sea spray, and seemed to be enjoying itself. Mark thought he heard a cry of joy.

The kelpie disappeared as it reached the bottom of the cliff, then shot upwards with an incredible force, it made Mark stagger back.

For all its speed, the kelpie landed gently, and let off its rider.

Harry.

The black horse's brittle blue eyes took in the scene of their destroyed home.

"Wh-what's happening here?" Harry asked, leaning comfortably against his kelpie friend. "Where did all the kids come from?"

Ah, so his new lover hadn't told him everything. "Coira has been taking them. Kelpies kidnap and eat children."

"What?"

"Don't listen to rumours. Don't let them villainise me." The kelpie said with its lovely Scottish tones.

"Harry, I need you to get out of here, it's not safe." Mark said, firmly. "Silvaticus, take Harry and the kids home."

A sea fog rolled in with unnatural speed, sweeping across the clifftop and turning the bright sun to night.

"No, Harry is mine. I won't let you take him from me." The kelpie hissed.

"Fine, I'll go with you. Just... don't hurt them." Harry pleaded, trying to get the kelpie's attention.

The kelpie gave an equine snort, ignoring the offer. Mark could feel the kelpie's dark magic reaching out to the water sources to fuel their spells. But there seemed to be something wrong.

The creature's ears flattened to its skull, giving an evil snake-like appearance; it's fangs bared.

Mark stared in amazement before it all clicked. Michelle had already claimed all the water and was blocking the kelpie from becoming more powerful.

His cousin was sweating with the exertion, but gave a smug smirk.

"We haven't met properly. I'm Michelle. The cool grandchild of the Grand High Witch." Michelle shook her head. "You should have took Harry's offer."

Mark quickly drew together a ball of fire, ready to throw it in the kelpie's direction, as soon as Harry got out of the bloody way.

"No, you can't hurt Coira." He growled.

The kelpie's cold blue eyes flicked between the witches, and the demon that sheltered the children. It was out-numbered.

And then everything froze.

Mark thought he heard music, it was hauntingly beautiful, and sung to all the hidden places within him. The fire he'd created died at his fingertips, and he found he couldn't move. He didn't want to move; he just wanted the song to go on forever.

He could just about sense Michelle, Silvaticus and the children all being frozen in this perfect moment with him. Their spells also faltered.

Mark could still see what was happening, he just couldn't process anything. He could see the kelpie accessing the water. He could see the darkness, the desire to kill, whilst their enemies were incapacitated.

"No!" Harry's scream broke through the perfect music, and made the rhythm falter enough for the spell to shift.

Harry was the only one not affected by the kelpie's spell – hadn't Coira said he was special?

Harry leapt in front of the spell, as the kelpie released it.

And crumpled to the ground.

Mark's heart shattered, and he threw off the remainder of the spell.

Fuelled by fear and anger, he called up the horse, which formed from the discarded rock. He threw fire into its heart and it burst to life; a fiery steed that charged down the kelpie.

With the creature knocked aside, Mark ran to Harry's side.

He threw himself onto his knees beside Harry. "He's not breathing." Mark shouted.

"Mark." Michelle's voice came, as she dashed closer.

"He's got no pulse." Mark said, feeling his friend's neck. "We - we need to do CPR."

"Mark, he's gone." Michelle's voice shook. "You saw the spell that hit him, there was no way to survive."

"NO." Mark shouted. "This is *Harry*."

"There's nothing-"

"It's Harry. I can't..." Mark stared down at his friend. He could feel the horse he'd created standing guard, its head lowered, ready to attack.

But the kelpie didn't seem to be retaliating. They were also stunned, and Mark could feel their pain radiate across the distance. They had loved Harry; and they had killed him.

"I can't live without him." Mark said, suddenly aware tears were streaming down his cheeks. "I won't. Together, we're powerful enough to create miracles. *Please* help me with one small miracle."

"You're a fool." Michelle snapped, but sat down across from Mark. "Silvaticus, get those bloody children back to their bloody parents. Now!"

The demon nodded, his eyes betraying the futility of their actions. He gathered the children close to him and opened the demon road. In a flash of white light, they vanished.

Mark felt the inviting calm of the circle he and Michelle created, but he didn't want to be comforted. He wanted the swirling emotions to continue, because if they stopped… everything would become real.

Mark looked up at the stone and fire horse he'd created. He'd breathed life into that, how was this any different?

He held Harry's hand. "Don't leave me." He pleaded.

Mark felt the power well between him and Michelle, it was so deep, Mark would have drowned, if it wasn't for his sole-minded intention. He felt a reluctance in the magic that he'd never noticed before, but he still poured it all into saving his friend.

And the magic just flowed through... and dissipated...

No, Mark couldn't lose him. His emotions were driven by the fire of anger and grief, and he screamed.

Mark felt someone touch his shoulder. Michelle was crying, and her nose was bleeding after pouring everything she had into Mark's experiment.

"I'm sorry." She murmured.

Mark felt blood run from his own nose, and wiped it away. He looked up at the kelpie, which hovered twenty metres away, its black body rippling with green light in time with its pain.

"You killed him." Mark shouted, his voice hoarse.

"You should never have interfered. Harry would have been immortal with me."

Mark looked to his fiery horse, which stood waiting patiently for commands. With a single thought, it dropped its head and charged at the kelpie, which gave a human scream, as steam rose from the contact.

Mark could feel Michelle casting beside him, pouring all of her fury into a storm, the wind picking up, and battering the kelpie.

The creature slumped to the ground, unable to stand against the onslaught.

"What's happening?" The words were so quiet, but they cut through the wild weather and crackling fire.

"Harry!" Mark ran back to find his best friend sitting up, looking confused, but unharmed.

There was a bright flash of white light, as the cavalry arrived.

Witches from Mark's coven appeared from the demon road; as did the MacGregor family, and Nanna holding a metal bridle.

Michelle let up her spell, and nodded to the others. "They're all yours."

Several of the witches looked mildly impressed by her magic, before they focussed on making a barrier, to stop the kelpie running away.

Nanna caressed the beautiful iron bridle that Derek had made for her at short notice, and moved towards the kelpie.

Her power radiated, but was unnecessary. Everyone could see the creature was beaten.

It almost seemed anti-climactic when Nanna slipped the bridle over the kelpies head.

The creature shuddered, and shifted, until it was Coira on their knees, with a new iron choker that laced about their delicate neck.

The MacGregors came forward.

"Well, that's got to be the easiest taming I've ever seen. Would you be open to working together in future?" The father, Ron asked.

Mark wasn't listening. It had been far from easy, and he'd been through the emotional ringer. "Take them away. I never want to see them again."

Chapter Nineteen

Silvaticus took everyone back to Denise's house. The MacGregors were the first to leave, with their prisoner obediently following them into their van.

In Mark's opinion, they couldn't take Coira far enough away to make him happy; but the Scottish Highlands was a start.

The witches were the next to go. They were both relieved and bemused at how easy today had been. They'd been drummed up, ready for action; but arrived to find the children already rescued, and the villain already stopped by the two youngest members of the coven. They waited to see if Nanna would need their service any further, but she seemed oddly distracted, and her second-in-command Denise insisted they head home.

"I think they were quite impressed." Denise said to Mark, after she ushered the last witch out. "You've proven you're capable of taking your Nanna's place next week."

"Thanks." Mark replied. He would have been relieved to hear that a month ago, but now he just felt numb.

"What happened?" Nanna asked, looking with a vague suspicion at Harry.

Mark relayed it all, his voice monotone and logically describing everything, because if he allowed emotion to enter for one moment, he didn't think he could stop it from crashing down.

Michelle filled in a few parts he'd missed.

Then the table sat in stunned silence.

"Harry, how do you feel?" Nanna asked gently.

"Dunno." Harry shrugged. "I feel fine. Bit embarrassed that Coira fooled me."

"Y-you said you knew they were a kelpie." Mark said quietly.

"Yeah, they made out they were some harmless water spirit." Harry blushed. "How dumb can I be?"

"Who knows that Harry died?" Nanna asked.

"Just the people in this room." Mark replied.

"And Coira. "Michelle added.

"Yeah, and them." Mark didn't even want to say their name.

"It's best we keep it that way. Tell no one, not even your parents." Nanna said, looking fiercely at the three teens in front of her. "Bringing someone back to life has no precedent. I don't want to bring the scrutiny and judgement of others until we've investigated this fully. Do you promise to keep this between us?"

"Yes." They all echoed.

"Good." Nanna stated, standing up. "It's been a long day. C'mon Harry, I'll give you a lift home."

Mark, Harry and Michelle all climbed into Nanna's old Landrover. She started up the engine, and for the first time ever, she drove sensibly, taking great care of her passengers.

The first stop was Harry's house. Nanna pulled up and helped him out.

"Now, if you have any weird feelings, or if you're bored and want to annoy him; please call Mark at any time of day or night." Nanna said with a smile.

Harry forced a laugh. "Sure thing, Nanna."

Mark watched his best friend disappear into his house, so utterly relieved that he'd managed to rescue him; but he had a haunting feeling that something bad was going to happen.

Nanna drove back to their house with her usual gusto. Mark clung to the armrest as he was flung around, finding the normality of it strangely settling. He quickly realised that Nanna's care was directed at Harry alone.

When they arrived home, they all managed to pile into Nanna's kitchen, before her anger exploded.

"WHAT WERE YOU THINKING?" She yelled, making the shelves around her shake. "YOU RAN BLINDLY INTO DANGER!"

"It wasn't blind." Mark argued, crossing his arms.

At the other side of the kitchen, Michelle gave him a look, declaring him crazy for standing up to Nanna right now.

"What is that supposed to mean?" Nanna asked, her fury barely controlled, as she tried to come across coldly.

"It means that I weighed up the risks and acted as necessary. With Harry gone, we thought that was the ninth child – we had to act before the kelpie killed them all." Mark nodded at his cousin. "Between me and Michelle, we're nearly as powerful as you, if not more so. We didn't want you to get hurt, so *we handled it.*"

Nanna crossed her arms, her eyes narrowing.

"I don't think you've accepted that you are stepping back. You're still in control of every little thing, and you don't want to let go." Mark snapped. "We're more than capable of doing our part, if you'd just loosen the reins a little."

"And just because you're taking on the Grand High Witch magic doesn't mean you suddenly have total authority." Nanna countered. "Especially when you so frequently show your lack of common sense!"

Mark was fuming. Adrenaline was running through him, and he wondered how much of this anger really needed to be directed at Nanna.

He jumped at the sound of the kettle clattering on top of the Aga. He turned to see Michelle making tea. It was such a mundane thing, but it made him pause.

"No, you two keep arguing. The house is still standing." Michelle taunted, as she got three cups down from the shelves that were still vibrating under Nanna's subconscious spell.

Nanna didn't say anything, but dropped her magic.

"I'm sorry Harry died, but you shouldn't have brought him back to life." Nanna eventually said, quietly.

Mark looked away from the pity in her eyes, before it made him cry. "You don't understand. It's Harry. I can't live without him, he's like a brother."

"I do understand. I've known that boy all his life, and I love him like family." Nanna's voice broke. "Bringing people back to life goes against nature."

"It's Harry." Mark replied weakly. "I would've done anything in that moment to save him; and I'd do it again."

Nanna took Mark's trembling hands. "Death is a natural part of life. Every person who dies, is special to someone, if they're lucky. Harry was loved, but he is no more above death than any other person. Just because you managed an impossible spell, does that mean you get to judge who lives and dies?"

Mark looked up, and was surprised to see his usually-strong Nanna crying. He tried to find words to speak, but his tongue was uncooperative. He shook his head.

"What will happen to Harry?" Michelle asked, setting down cups of tea in front of them.

212

"I don't know." Nanna wiped the tears from her cheeks. "You've done natural magic that I thought was impossible. I've only ever seen dark magic bring people back to life – although they were shadows of their former selves and servants of the necromancers who raised them…"

"I didn't use dark magic." Mark promised.

"I know." Nanna said, patting his hand. "But it doesn't mean there won't be some pretty serious consequences. You'll need to keep a close eye on him. Let me know if any odd behaviours arise – well, odd for Harry."

Chapter Twenty

The next day, Mark cycled over to Harry's house, his heart heavy, and his limbs weary after the massive use of magic.

He knew the route off by heart, but it seemed to take twice as long this morning, and Mark was exhausted by the end of the ride, reminiscent of his dark magic hangover. He'd definitely pushed himself too much yesterday, but he'd do it all over again, if he had to.

Mark knocked on the door, which was answered by Harry's mum.

"Oh, Mark, just the person. Harry's feeling a bit down, I think he and Coira broke up." Mrs Johnson looked amused at the lifespan of a teenage relationship. "He'll be pleased to see you. Do you want to take some cans of pop up to his room?"

"Yes, Mrs Johnson." Mark said, trying to put on a polite smile.

He grabbed a couple of cokes from the fridge, and headed upstairs. He found Harry sitting in his room in silence, his best friend staring out the window.

"Hey."

Mark's greeting made Harry jump. "Oh, hey mate."

Mark handed over one of the cans and sat on the chair with the least amount of clothes on. He was surprised how quiet it was – Harry religiously listened to music, it was always in the background, no matter what. It seemed eerie without it.

"No music today?" Mark asked, wanting to avoid the serious questions for a little longer.

Harry shook his head. "No, I don't know if I ever want to listen to it again. Coira always used to say every song had a story, and every story has power... I just hear *them* every time I listen to music."

Mark sighed, so much for the easy question. "I'm sorry."

"It's not your fault." Harry said.

"It is. I was the idiot that broke someone out of a demon prison, of all places." Mark played with the can. "They just seemed so innocent; I didn't question it."

"I think that's part of Coira's charm. They drew everyone in." Harry said dully. "I still can't believe they were gonna eat those kids!"

"It was their nature." Mark said. "I was scared they were gonna eat you, too. When I found that you weren't with the missing kids, I was terrified. I had no idea what they were up to."

"Um, we went for a ride. Coira wanted to share one of their favourite parts of being a kelpie. They had such honest excitement for such simple things – singing, and the sea…" Harry blushed. "And they were really a monster all along."

"If it makes you feel any better, I think they really did love you. They were distraught when… well…"

"No, it doesn't make me feel better." Harry snorted. "I still feel like an idiot getting involved with Coira. Especially after the hard time I've given you about the demons."

"Yeah, I think we're about equal on being played for a fool." Mark said, not meeting Harry's gaze.

"I think I knew that it was wrong on some level. I've never kept secrets from you in my life, and suddenly I'm spending all my time with a magical water spirit." Harry sighed. "But I felt like Coira was put in this world for me. They were perfect, and they were all mine…"

"I'm sorry." Mark repeated quietly.

The two guys sat in silence for what felt like forever.

"Are you still alright, physically?" Mark asked.

Harry shrugged. "I feel weird. You know when you can't get comfortable. I didn't really sleep good last night, so I'm a bit tired. But I've got no desire to drink blood, or eat brains, so I think I'm alright."

Mark gave a pity laugh.

"I'd rather not be a zombie, if I get my pick." Harry mused. "I mean, apart from Warm Bodies, they're kinda the losers of the undead posse."

"Ah, well your jokes aren't any better now that you're not-dead." Mark replied in good spirit.

Harry went silent again, looking out the window.

"Thank you, for saving me."

Mark nodded, and gazed out the window, too, as tears threatened to fall. He might have been wrong to bring his friend back to life, but he was going to do everything he could to make sure Harry was safe and happy.

"There's, um… something I want to talk to you about." Mark said.

"Uh-oh, this sounds serious. Is it on par with dying?" Harry asked.

"Erm, no. Hopefully nothing will ever be on par with that again." Mark frowned, not sure if he should laugh at his friend's comment. "It's about Lughnasadh."

"I'm still allowed to come, aren't I?"

"Yes, of course." Mark replied quickly. "No, what I want to speak to you about is… I am taking on the Grand High Witch powers. It's time, and I can't keep putting it off."

"I know. You're ready."

"Thanks. Um, well, when I'm this super-powerful witch, I'll no longer need a protective spirit." Mark said. "I'll no longer be able to summon Luka. So, I was wondering if you'd like to take him on?"

"But, how? I'm not a witch." Harry asked, not wanting to get his hopes up. "I can't sustain the spell."

"Yeah, but I've been experimenting with my magic lately. I think I can make him real." Mark closed his eyes and called on his protective spirit.

The black-and-white collie appeared in Harry's bedroom, and seeing no danger at hand, he curled up on the floor.

Mark kept his eyes closed. He could sense the spirit, and could feel their joy at being a permanent part of their world. Mark reached out for his magic, and wove it into the shape of the dog. He then pushed fire into the heart, giving it the spark of life.

"Your nose is bleeding!" Harry exclaimed, pushing some tissues towards him.

Mark sighed. "It's nothing. I just pushed myself too much last night, I'm still feeling it now."

"Did it work?" Harry asked, excited.

Mark nodded, not trusting himself to speak. He watched as Harry made a massive fuss of his new dog, laughing as Luka licked his face enthusiastically.

"I'd best get home." Mark said quietly. He got up, then turned back, giving Luka one more fuss behind the ears. "Thank you, for everything, Luka. You'll have a good life here."

Mark left Harry's house, and was surprised to see Robert waiting outside for him. Filled with embarrassment over the last time they met, Mark slunk over, with his hands in his pockets.

"Hey." He greeted.

"Hello." Robert said, his dark eyes worried. "I had to check on you. Miriam told us that Harry got kidnapped by the kelpie last night… I thought you might be here."

"Thank you, I appreciate it."

"Damian also wanted to come, but I won the fight for control." Robert said.

If Mark didn't know him better, he'd think that the usually-confident demon was prattling.

"Are you alright?" Robert asked so gently, that it nearly made Mark cry.

"I've screwed up." He blinked back the tears. "I've screwed up so many times. I nearly lost Harry last night, and it was all my fault. I should've listened to you about the kelpie, and I shouldn't have argued with you."

"Oh, Mark. You made the best choice you could in the demon realm, it's one of your more frustrating noble qualities." Robert said, his backward compliment missing his usual hidden meanings. "I know I wasn't there last night, but I'm sure you did the same."

"I'm… sorry for what I said last time I saw you. I should never have sent you away. If I hadn't…" Mark bit his lip.

"You can't change the past. Trust me, I've tried." Robert said with a bitter smile.

"Yes, but Coira… um, hurt Harry. And I was so mad with them, for daring to endanger someone I care for. We had them beat, but I didn't want to stop. A part of me wanted to kill them, for what they'd done. I knew that it was within my power." Mark swallowed, the guilt lacing through him painfully. "If Nanna and the rest of the coven hadn't come at that moment, I don't know what I would have done…"

Robert grabbed him firmly by his arms, forcing Mark to look at him. "Thinking about killing, and actually doing the deed are a million miles apart. You are a good guy. I think we can both agree you've got a long way to fall before you become a monster like me."

"I just… couldn't help thinking that we weren't so different. I could relate to the darkness. The lengths we went to for the ones that we…" Mark broke off. "I'm sorry I betrayed your trust. I promise I'll never use your name in that manner again."

Mark leant forward and kissed the demon that loved him.

Chapter Twenty-One

The first of August brought Lughnasadh, one of the big fire festivals, this one marking the start of the harvest.

Lughnasadh had always been a fun, family event; but this year it carried more importance.

Mark noted that the witches from the coven came to greet him, as well as Nanna when they arrived. Their manner was so very different to the Summer Solstice, when they'd practically snubbed the lad.

Denise must be right – they were all impressed with how he and Michelle had (almost-)single-handedly rescued those children and subdued the kelpie. Actions always did speak louder than words.

The coven had always been pleasant to him, but this was the first time they made him feel positive about taking over Nanna's role.

Nanna was somewhere at the party, Mark wasn't sure where exactly. After their little argument, she and Mark had been a little distant. Oh, they'd both apologised, but Mark suspected she felt like he did – licking her wounds from the accusations that had a little truth to them.

He'd spied Derek and his nephew arrive earlier – both had been invited this time. He was sure that the farrier had been pulled to his Nanna like gravity.

The farrier might have been falling for Nanna previously; but after being part of the team that freed the kids, providing the kelpie bridle... Mark now suspected he was a lost cause, and would never leave her side.

When Harry arrived with his parents, Mark was happier than he thought he'd be, that Harry brought Luka.

The collie had his very own collar, and Harry carried a lead that he'd probably never have to use on the intelligent creature.

Harry's parents both had a bemused look, still not sure how they suddenly became dog owners.

Mark gave Luka a fuss, glad he'd done one thing right in his recent run of mistakes.

"You alright?" Mark asked.

Harry winced. "Yeah, you?"

"Yeah, 'bout there." Mark replied, earning him a very sharp elbow in his ribs.

Damian arrived shortly after, and Mark went to meet him. It was the first time he'd seen his boyfriend since the fight with the kelpie.

Mark had put off visits, claiming he was tired; but he was just putting it off. He didn't like to have secrets from Damian. He couldn't tell him about Harry getting killed, because Nanna had forbidden them. And he definitely couldn't tell him about Robert.

Mark was more confused than ever. Standing in front of Damian, he was more in love with him than ever. Losing Harry had made Mark appreciate him so much more.

But he couldn't deny he felt *something* for Robert.

His lips burnt with the memory of their kiss. He'd been surprised, expecting the passionate demon to kiss him hard and fast… but instead, it had been slow and full of promise, as though he had the whole of eternity to see him satisfied.

When midnight drew near, most of the non-witches drifted away; leaving just the coven and their families.

The witches stood in a circle around the bonfire. Mark noted how very different the atmosphere was, to the last time they'd done this circle. That had been in the middle of winter, with the purpose of rejecting an evil demon. This time, it was officially welcoming Michelle to their family; and marking the chosen heir taking their place.

As soon as Mark stepped into line, he felt the warm acceptance of his magical family. Curious, he looked over to Michelle, and saw that she was nearly overcome. The broken witch who had made a deal with the devil to get a family, finally had a bigger one than she could have dreamt.

The coven started to chant as one, and Mark felt the words ring through him:

"Through the mists of time and space;

"Through locks and walls, to this set place.

"We call upon the ancient power;

"Greeted at the midnight hour.

"Link our hopes and hearts as one;

"Til our intentions be done."

The steady strength of his family reached out and soothed his troubles, making him truly smile for the first time in days.

Nanna came forward and took his hand, leading him closer to the fire.

She took out a knife, and cut her hand as she spoke.

"I was the guardian;

"I was the servant;

"I have been the steady guide.

"My time is done, and I pass on this duty with an open heart."

Mark could see the blood from the cut shimmer with gold, and he wondered if it was a trick of the firelight.

He took the knife from Nanna, and copied her actions.

"I am the guardian;

"I am the servant;

"I will be the steady guide.

"From today, until my last, I accept this duty with an open heart."

Nanna smiled, and placed their bloody hands together.

"Thank you." She murmured.

And then the rush happened…

Other books by K.S. Marsden:

Witch-Hunter ~ *Now available in audiobook*
The Shadow Rises (Witch-Hunter #1)
The Shadow Reigns (Witch-Hunter #2)
The Shadow Falls (Witch-Hunter #3)

Witch-Hunter trilogy box-set

Witch-Hunter Prequels
James: Witch-Hunter (#0.5)
Sophie: Witch-Hunter (#0.5)
Kristen: Witch-Hunter (#2.5) ~ *coming soon*

Enchena
The Lost Soul: Book 1 of Enchena
The Oracle: Book 2 of Enchena

Northern Witch
Winter Trials (Northern Witch #1)
Awaken (Northern Witch #2)
The Breaking (Northern Witch #3)
Summer Sin (Northern Witch #4)
A Dark Fate (Northern Witch #5)

Printed in Great Britain
by Amazon